I0654003

THE GIRL CAGE

THE GIRL CAGE

CHARLES MERGENDAHL

CUTTING EDGE

Copyright © 1953 Charlies Mergendahl

This was later republished under the title *The Lonely Ones*

The characters and events portrayed in this book are fictitious. Any similarity to real persons, living or dead, is coincidental and not intended by the author. No part of this book may be reproduced, or stored in a retrieval system, or transmitted in any form or by any means, electronic, mechanical, photocopying, recording, or otherwise, without express written permission of the publisher.

ISBN-13: 978-1-962896-49-8

Published by
Cutting Edge Books
PO Box 8212
Calabasas, CA 91372
www.cuttingedgebooks.com

CHAPTER ONE

T HERE WERE thick clouds that afternoon, so the sun was only a dying light bulb, and the ships looked weirdly black as they moved slowly down to the horizon and beyond to that strange land across the sea.

I watched the passing ships from a halfway point on the steep hill that boasts San Diego's El Cortez Hotel. I had watched those ships before, those and many others—destroyers and carriers and battleships and troop ships—and as it happened with the other wives in San Diego, those passing ships brought me somehow closer to my husband, merely because only a sea—though thousands of miles across—only the Pacific lay there between us.

A whistle sounded behind me. I started and jerked my eyes to the face of the sailor who strode expectantly toward me from across the street. "Looking for someone, baby? Going somewhere, baby?"

"No." I smiled wearily, and continued the long climb. I wasn't looking for him, not for any of the other leering sailors, not for the young soldiers who passed in a jeep, craning their necks to see me as they passed. I wasn't looking for anyone except a man named Phil, who was now somewhere in Korea, across those miles of water. I wasn't going anywhere except up to the El Cortez for a quiet drink and a few hours' break from the monotonous life I'd been enduring for the nine months since Phil had gone.

I quickened my step. The hat box I carried swung in against my legs, and after a moment I sat down on a stone bench to rest. The hat box was light enough, but I was annoyed with it because I did not want the absurd hat so carefully wrapped in tissue, so neatly placed inside. I'd bought it only minutes before—a black thing with a veil and a pale blue feather, all supposed to symbolize the great adventure. The big splurge. Martha Gwynn, age twenty-three, had taken a bus from the town of Salamanca to the city of San Diego, a distance of exactly twelve miles. And on this, her first excursion in months, she had bought a hat that cost exactly sixteen dollars. Of course she didn't normally wear hats at all, and as a matter of fact, her husband didn't even like her in hats. But since her husband was a good five thousand miles away, and since a hat, any hat, was the sign of a woman's rebellion against routine, well, Martha Gwynn had bought a hat.

Very exciting. I tried to smile at how ridiculously dull this supposedly special day had been. But the smile would not come. The sea was too sullen, the afternoon too late, the El Cortez too high above me. And as I moved on again, even faster now, I concentrated on the people around me—the indolent sailors and hip-swinging girls, the quickly-joined couples who laughed and owned the city, and owned each other for just a little while. And I tried to imagine myself holding Phil's arm as we walked through the city and laughed together. We had done that once in San Francisco and ... but then I shook my head and plodded on toward the single cocktail I'd been promising myself since very early morning.

Yet Phil walked with me still, from that other hill in those months before. And nearing the top of the steep incline, I remembered it all in spotty detail. San Francisco's Mark Hopkins at the peak of Nob Hill, and the Top-of-the-Mark with the same big glass windows that looked out on the bridge and the harbor and the ships moving in and out from sea. I remembered sitting there by the huge window on Phil's last night before sailing, saying nothing, while his stubby fingers touched mine with secret meaning before we rose together and I followed him to the elevator, looking straight ahead as we went down together and walked stiffly to our room, where we undressed with careful deliberate motions, expressing nothing until our bodies touched and the awkwardness disappeared—until I wanted nothing but to arch myself against him and say, "Don't go, please don't go," with my eyes closed and the long-stoppered tears squeezing out at the corners.

I shook my head, then stood motionless, breathing heavily after the long climb. The entrance to the El Cortez was directly ahead, and behind was that same gray sea and those black ships crawling down over the horizon. Nine months ago, I told myself. It was nine months ago. And I continued on through the glass doors, into the lobby, across the tiled floor, as though I were doing it all over again, only doing it alone now. I waited alone by the elevator. Inside I stood alone facing the elevator boy's back, remembering how I'd gone up alone to the Top-of-the-Mark on that very last night of all. Then the door slid open and I stepped alone into the high cocktail lounge with the windows familiar from that other time, the circular bar familiar, everything familiar from that other lost time—even the uniformed backs of the noisy drinkers and the little tables along the circular glass wall.

The room was full, but I hardly noticed. A waiter approached, saying words that I did not hear. I moved slowly around the bar, thinking carefully that it was left. Yes, it *had* been left. Phil had come up ahead of me while I'd been dressing, and I'd found him at the third table down on the left. This table right here by the window. He'd picked up his glass and said, "Here's the go," and—and then he'd turned to look at me and—and there he was now, sitting alone, waiting, picking up his glass, sipping, putting the glass down again, looking up, smiling, rising a little, saying, "Well—hello—"

CHAPTER TWO

T HIS WAS THE El Cortez Hotel in San Diego. Not the Mark Hopkins in San Francisco. This man was a lieutenant in the navy and not in the army, and not Phil, but rather a tall man with a lean, almost haunted face, brown hair that would not stay in place, a slightly hooked nose, and a smile that touched only the corners of his mouth. He said, "Hello again," then looked at the hat box in my hand and said, "Hank McKellar's buying drinks for all blonde girls with hat boxes and a lost look about them."

I stared down at the hat box, then out to sea, across the darkness to that land somewhere.

"Of course if you'd rather drink standing up ..."

"No—" I swung my eyes back to his. "I wasn't thinking of—"

"You like the height. You're trying to overcome a bad case of that fear of high places."

"Acrophobia."

A shadow crossed his unsmiling face. "All right," he said. "Acrophobia." Then he looked away from me, angry, leaving me to stay or go with no more bantering of words. I felt I should say something. Goodbye, or something. I'm sorry, or something. "That drink," I said finally.

"I offered it. If you want it, sit down and I'll offer it again."

"Well—" And after a moment I sat down across from him, placing the box on the floor beside my chair. "As a matter of fact—"

"As a matter of fact?" His eyes had turned toward me again. They were set off by bleached lashes and those tiny crowfoot lines that mark a man who is at home with all kinds of weather. I noticed the steady eyes. And then I did not look at him again. I looked at my own nervous fingers touching the paper napkin, folding it into a paper hat.

"Nothing," I said. "I—I was startled, that's all. You see I've never been up here before, but I have been to the Top-of-the-Mark and—"

"And it jarred you because they're so much alike."

"Yes—even this table. I sat at a table just where this one is, and—"

"With your husband." It was not a question, but a statement in a low voice, while his eyes dropped to my wedding ring.

"Yes...." I studied the gold ring. I turned it between my fingers. Phil, I thought. Phil ... Phil. And I rose abruptly. But he was holding out a cigarette. I took it without thinking. He lighted it for me, then turned sharply to look out the big windows and wait for the drinks to arrive. I hesitated, puzzled, unsure of myself. Then I sat down again and balanced the paper hat on my nervous finger. The drinks came and he raised his glass and looked at me, saying, "To your husband."

"Phil."

"And to Phil's wife."

"Martha. Martha Gwynn." Our glasses touched, but I was thinking only of Phil again—how we'd met like this and touched glasses like this—how we'd gone down to our room and—

"Here's the go," he said.

Suddenly my hand shook and I set the glass down so the drink spilled, soaking into the paper hat. "Don't say that! Please don't say that!"

"All right." He watched me calmly. He waited, then asked me simple questions in a direct, almost authoritative voice. How old was I? Twenty-three. How long had I been married? Almost two years. Where was I born? Sadler Falls, New Hampshire. Question after question until after a while I caught myself answering questions he had not even asked, telling him something about my personal self and about Phil, and about being here in San Diego alone after nine months in the nearby town of Salamanca.

"I don't know why I chose Salamanca particularly. It's a pretty town, and—"

"And near Korea."

"Yes ... I suppose it does sound a little silly. But Phil will come in on the West Coast, you see, and after all I'm not the only wife who feels the same way. There're five of us in the house where I live. Really it's a sort of cottage. Belongs to Lloyd Watkins, a wealthy dilettante who lets us use his guest house rent free. It overlooks the beach—very beautiful—and the main house where Lloyd lives is all glass and brick and—"

"And it's so beautiful that you couldn't stand it any longer, so you decided to run away."

"No...." I paused, finished the cocktail, and had scarcely put down the glass before the waiter set another in its place. And then, lifting the glass carefully for that first sip, then suddenly I wanted to explain my theory, Martha Gwynn's big theory about Hope, Martha Gwynn's conviction that it isn't false hope at all that keeps a prisoner alive, but the fierce attention to the moment—to the coffee you drink, the cigarette you smoke, the brushing of your hair, the putting on of lipstick—all with an intense concentration that makes something alive in a dead prisoner's life. Yet in my own case the physical details of every-day living were so terribly comfortable that somehow they were painfully disturbing. That was what I wanted to say. But the only words that came out were, "Attention to detail—that's the way—"

"Until," he said ironically, "you start wanting different details."

"Yes, I guess that's it." I was concentrating on the olive in my half-empty martini glass. I ate it slowly, and then in a moment I was concentrating on the face of Lieutenant Hank McKellar. He was looking out the window, and in that nearly homely profile I saw none of the good-natured easy-come-and-go of other naval officers I'd met at various parties around Salamanca. There was an intensity in the line of his jaw, the high cheekbones, the thin mouth that showed defiance—the kind of intensity that probably made him a good naval officer, and could, were the cards stacked in a different way, make him an unbearable man.

He caught my reflection in the dark glass. "You don't seem like the other lonely wives I've met."

"Don't I?"

"No, they were—"

"I know. Yes, I know." And I dropped it there. For I did not want to talk about my housemates or the hundred or so other waiting wives I met each day on the beach below our adobe cottage—jealous, bored, frustrated, drinking too much and sleeping around too much. "They want too much," I said aloud, "I guess I'm a sort of mother confessor. Good little girl from small town, New Hampshire. Married there, with a big excursion to Westchester. Phil was an assistant account representative for an advertising agency, so we lived in Westchester, you see, and— well, it was all very ordered and proper and—"

"Satisfying."

"Yes—satisfying." I picked up the nearly finished cocktail. He turned from the window and watched me carefully, his eyes focused plainly on my mouth. I put the glass to my lips and kept it there a long time, hiding behind the glass, waiting for him to look away. The glass was empty when I finally set it down.

I laughed, but the laughter was hollow. It seemed to hang there between us, echoing in the empty glasses. "What about you?"

"Me?"

"Where are you from and what do you do and all that sort of thing?"

"Merchant Marine." He spoke curtly as though trying to say as little and get it over with as quickly as possible. "Then this destroyer duty with the navy. I was in the navy during the last war, and now I'm back again. So that's what about me."

"Yes, but—"

"That's what about me."

"I see."

"I don't think there's anything else you'd like to hear about." His voice was harsh when he spoke. Two fingers of his lean hand gripped the rim of his martini glass; two others were clamped low on the stem. "Except," he said, "except sometimes men get lonesome too." Then he laughed without humor and his fingers jerked, breaking the martini glass clearly across the middle of the stem. A trickle of blood started down his index finger.

"You've cut yourself." I said it automatically, then let my voice die away. I looked at the thin line of blood and I lit a cigarette with a trembling hand.

We were silent. Darkness crept outside the window. The ships had lost their shapes, and were nothing but tiny blinking lights on the black sea. An occasional highflying gull soared on the wind outside. A sailor staggered by. He was drunk, holding onto the tables. He bumped against my chair and apologized, then looked at the lieutenant and said, "Sorry, Mr. McKellar," and, "She's sure a beautiful lady, Mr. McKellar."

"Thank you, Mike." He smiled suddenly at the sailor. "You ought to have one yourself."

"I sure as hell should." And the sailor stared at me with bleary eyes before he finally nodded and lurched off toward the elevator.

"Mike," Hank McKellar said. "A good man with a twenty-millimeter gun."

"He likes you," still watching the blood on his hand. "I think maybe all your men like you."

"Do blondes with hat boxes like me?" He was laughing again, but with a touch of humor now. "I'm buying dinner for blondes with hat boxes."

"No, I—"

"Not here. Nowhere in this hotel."

"Oh...." I paused, confused, then started to object again. But when I glanced at his eyes, I knew in that moment that he understood—perhaps more than I understood myself.

So I agreed to have dinner with Lieutenant Hank McKellar. To this day I can't explain exactly why. Because I'd come to San Diego for this very purpose—to meet someone different and do something gay. Because somehow, in the odd way that we'd met, my loneliness and longing for Phil had expressed itself without my even speaking. And finally, simply because I was a girl—lonely, dressed-up, bored, and with nowhere to go. It's impossible to give one clear reason why something is done impulsively. It's done because you want to do it. Even if you argue violently before giving in, it's still done for the same reason—because you want to do it.

So I went to dinner with Hank McKellar. I followed him to the elevator, noticing how he stooped a little as he walked, trying to guess at his age, wondering why it should make any difference who or what he was, so long as he tried to be pleasant and we both enjoyed ourselves.

Getting into the elevator he touched my arm, and then with only the two of us there in the dropping cage, then the feeling was back again, and once again I was going down to that bedroom in the Mark Hopkins, rushing toward a deliberate undressing and—I squeezed my eyes together tight, opened them slowly on Hank McKellar's hand, on the fingers that were strong and stained with blood, on the nails that were unmanicured.

He clenched the hand into a fist. "What's in the hat box?" he said quietly.

"Guess." I pulled back to the forced gaiety of reality.

"A hat. I'll bet you're terrific in a hat."

And it was good he'd said that, because it was exactly the opposite of what Phil would have said. It snapped me securely into the present, though my voice trailed on about the past. "Nine months ago. It was nine months ago." I noticed that he did not answer. I noticed that he frowned a little and walked a trifle faster when we crossed the lobby.

But going through the revolving door—then I was finally free, able to laugh naturally and keep pace with the striding Lieutenant Hank McKellar.

He smiled and said, "We'll never go there any more."

"We?"

"Us. We'll go other places, but not to the El Cortez." He hailed a cab, sat far back in his corner, and smoked one cigarette after another while we drove down the hill and through the city. And he talked a great deal of nonsense over further cocktails and an abalone steak dinner in a small seafood restaurant near the waterfront. I'd been in many restaurants that were much the same. Yet somehow here the candlelight was softer, the wine more pleasant, and even the little man with his violin, moving from table to table—-even he was something new and quaint, as though I were having dinner like this for the very first time in my life.

"Do you come here often?" I asked.

"Never before." His pale eyes were steady through the flickering candlelight. "Never before," as though it were very important that this was the first time for both of us. "And the name," he said, "the name is Hank,"

"Hank." I said it twice, but I was not looking at him.

"As a matter of fact," he said, still looking at me, "I feel this is a celebration of some kind. You bought a new hat and I met Martha Gwynn." His voice was flat. The words had no meaning, as though he were reciting lines that he'd repeated many times before. He drank then, and carefully broke off a piece of Italian bread with his rough fingers. "So where do we go from here?"

"Home, I think, I'd better—"

"I'm talking to myself."

"Oh...." And I asked myself the same question. "Where do we go from here? And why is the familiarity here again, now after we've left the El Cortez?" I looked at the back of Hank's hand lying flat on the table, the blood dry and crusty along the cut finger. Then I glanced up at his mouth, crooked in the corners, opening slightly while his tongue ran slowly around his thin lips. The cocktails, I told myself. They distort things. But I'm a big girl now, and I'm going to stop worrying and just enjoy myself.

We had drambuie following dinner, and we went other places in the lighted city. We drank scotch highballs, and both admitted that we felt like drinking. And for a while there it was almost gay—and almost wonderful. I forgot Hank's bursts of angry intensity. I even forgot my housemates and my own boredom and even Phil for a small harmless while. And suddenly I wanted this strange man to know how I honestly felt about this particular day. But I think he knew, though I tried to say it anyway. "You know, I'm having a wonderful time. The best in months."

"That's good."

"And you know I—I sort of hope I won't remember in the morning."

Only the twitching muscles of his face showed he understood what I meant. And watching him in the dimmed light, I wondered if I really understood myself.

Hank insisted on driving me back to the guest house, though first we'd take a cab to his ship, where he could borrow a jeep. "Maybe you'd like to come aboard. Have a look at the sailor's life."

"Well—"

"Maybe you'll put on that new hat."

I did not answer. He'd said *maybe*, yet he'd meant it as an order. And I wondered why I did not resent him.

The destroyer sat low in the water, covered with paint-splattered canvas and coils of twisting rubber hose. A young ensign nodded, then saluted as we came aboard. Two sailors sat playing cards under a gun. Another wearing only dungarees lay back against a bulkhead. He was drinking coffee from a white mug; a worn comic book lay face down in his lap. He glanced up, and his eyes widened before he turned away. He was young, and he watched me closely as I passed.

"They call him 'Baby,'" Hank said. "He's hardly seventeen, from Tennessee. A nice boy who doesn't know what to do with himself."

"I thought every sailor—"

"He's used to seeing women in bare feet. He gets scared in the city." His voice was lost in the sudden staccato of steel hammering steel. There was noise everywhere, echoing through the ship, pounding in my ears. "Air hammers. They work at night." Hank was shouting then. "It's impossible to sleep here !"

I nodded, wondering where he did sleep. Then he moved off and I followed him along the deck, stepping over the snake-black rubber hose. He showed me the wardroom and the bridge. He showed me the open door to his small cabin, and told me to wait there while he arranged for the jeep. "Put on the hat," he said. "Have it on when I get back."

Then he was gone and I was alone in the tiny cabin—alone with the noise that pounded inside my head, bringing pain and angry thoughts.

Who does he think he is? and where do we go from here, boys, oh where do we go from here?

And I knew gradually that this day had been familiar because this day had happened before at another time. In Sadler Falls, New Hampshire, with Phil, in the quiet of a country roadhouse. There'd been no anger, no noise, no drinks but coffee—completely different and in a way exactly the same. A first meeting as this was a first meeting. A beginning as this was a ...

I sat down in the narrow bunk, hugging the hat box to my knees. I stared at Hank's razor on the wash basin, at his worn khakis hanging in the open locker. I lit a match and studied the two photos on the locker door. One was Hank himself, younger then, seated proudly behind the wheel of a small fishing sloop. The other was one of those standardized photos of a naked girl in one of those standardized poses. The match burned my finger. I dropped it, swore, and then suddenly I ripped open the hat box, took out the black velvet hat with the pale blue feather and the thin black veil. I perched the hat on my head, adjusted it in the tiny mirror over the metal wash basin. Every move was automatic, done without thought or reason. My lips were dry, and my face looked entirely different under the veil. It was the face of someone I had not really noticed for a very long time. An ordinary face, I thought then—the hair blond, sun-bleached, the skin brown, the eyes very blue and very pale.

Only the upper part of my body was visible in the glass. But I could see the full bust and the waist that was almost ridiculously small. "Put my arm all the way around it." Phil had said that on our last night together in our room at the Mark Hopkins. "Don't lose a pound, baby, not a pound." And he'd stared at me very hard so that I'd become embarrassed with his frank eyes wandering over me as I lay nearly naked on the bed. I'd pulled a sheet to my chin and Phil had laughed. Then he'd jerked away the sheet, and afterwards we'd gone down in the elevator together and across the town together. And we'd stood together on the wooden dock until he'd pulled away and walked up the ship's gangway and completely out of my life.

"All set?" The voice startled me. I turned, leaning back against the metal basin, watching Hank's face in the half dark. It was more intense than ever. There was something fierce behind his eyes. His hand moved out and his rough fingers touched the edge of the veil. "Got on your armor," he said. And it was strange how I could hear his whisper above the echoing noise.

"My first hat in a long time. Phil doesn't like them on me, so—"

"I like them on you." He emphasized the *I* as though it made some difference, and then his fingers lifted the veil slowly, careful not to tear it. "Not bad. You've a pretty nice face. Good figure. Maybe the waist too small," talking like a callous judge at an Atlantic City beauty contest.

"Thank you, Lieutenant." I tried to laugh. My back was pressed hard against the metal wash basin and the noise of the air hammers kept drumming into my brain. One of Hank's fingers touched my cheek as he lifted the veil clear. It was the cut finger, and the rough scrape of dried blood sent a shock into my throat, so I jerked away and said, "Thank you, thank you, thank you!" I was shouting then, raising my voice above the deafening noise. And I was still saying those meaningless words when the hammers stopped abruptly so that my voice went on, echoing on the steel walls of the tiny cabin. "Thank you, thank you—" I stopped. "I'm sorry," I whispered.

"What's the matter with you?" He had sat on the bunk. He lit a cigarette, blew smoke into the room. "A guy likes you in a hat and you have a nervous breakdown."

I did not answer, but slowly then, standing there awkwardly in the blue smoke of his cigarette, I began to dislike Lieutenant Hank McKellar. He had recognized that odd second of desire between two people who had met only hours before. And he might, in that passing second—he might have kissed me. And afterwards, who knows? I might have been angry, and I might have laughed and I might have forgotten. But Hank McKellar had kept himself firmly in the driver's seat. He had meant me to feel like a priggish fool.

"I wasn't trying to sleep with you," he said.

"Oh, my God!"

"I don't like to try things with the odds against me." And I laughed then, for in that moment he sounded like a few boys I had known in college. They told you what they would not try in order to prepare themselves for the trying.

"She's a cinch," I said, talking very fast now, trying to cover my quick embarrassment. "This time I got her lined up. Just lined her up, fellas. And here's a big wink and let's have another glass of beer with the brothers of old Alpha Pi."

"Cut that out!" His voice was low, and he meant it. And looking through the half dark at his stiffening body, I realized finally that Mr. Hank McKellar had not gone to college and Mr. Hank

McKellar usually meant what he said. There were no games here, and I was to blame for thinking there ever could be.

"I've cut it out," I said. Then I turned and strode out of the cabin and along the deck. The hate fell as I moved, but I did not pick it up. I passed the young sailor from Tennessee and threw him a weak smile. "Hello, Baby," I said, and felt his watchful eyes on my back. I nodded to the deck officer, and went down the creaking gangway and climbed into the jeep that waited on the dock. I was breathing hard. My head was still filled with the beating hammers, and blood was pounding in my throat.

CHAPTER THREE

I T SEEMED HOURS before Hank got into the jeep beside me. The veiled hat was in his hand. "You dropped it," he said.

"I don't like it anyway." And the pounding was still there in my dry throat.

"You mean you don't like it *any more.*"

"I never did."

"Well—" He started the engine and drove fast along the dock, past the sleeping ships and the warehouses and the sailors singing drunkenly as they returned from town, on through the town itself to the open road. Neither of us spoke. The air was warm against my face and the jeep's tires made a tiny hum on the black macadam.

Salamanca was asleep when we drove through the main street. The shop windows were dark except for an occasional night light in the rear of a jewelry store. The sidewalks were empty except for an occasional marine or sailor who staggered uncertainly toward a single waiting bus.

"I've heard of this town," Hank said. "A streamlined cesspool."

"Everything," I murmured. "Everything becomes stagnant if it sits long enough."

"You're telling me!" He followed my directions through the residential district to the long gravel drive that led up to the main house of Lloyd Watkins. "So that's where you live," Hank said, his eyes studying the columns on either side of the drive.

"No, in a guest house beyond the trees. That's Lloyd Watkins' place. We're on his property."

"I see."

"He's been very kind."

"Payment deferred."

"What does that mean?"

"Nothing." He smiled a little. "You told me it was rent free."

He'd trapped me again and I felt the anger returning. "All right," I said. "Touché and goodnight."

"I'll drive you—"

"I'll walk. And thank you for a very nice time." There was a touch of irony in my voice. I didn't know whether I wanted it there or not. "Thanks," I said, and it could have meant anything.

"You're not taking the hat?"

"No."

"I'll keep it."

"If you like."

"Martha—"

"I had a very nice time."

"Oh, where do we go from here, boys?"

I looked at his face. Hard, disagreeable, his nose slightly hooked, his lips a straight line. "Goodnight," I said. Then I turned and walked fast up the drive, past the main house with the windows yellow in the moonlight, through the hawthorn and avacado and eucalyptus trees and past the empty swimming pool to the adobe cottage.

The house was dark, but I did not turn on the lights. I knew every square inch of that living room—the fieldstone fireplace to the left of the doorway, the swinging kitchen door beyond, the tiny hallway to the right. I knew the location of all the bamboo furniture, and knew also how now, at this time of night, it would be disarranged. A guitar would be lying on the sofa. It was, vibrating under my groping fingers. A wet bathing suit would be dripping on the hearth, though no fire had burned there in months. The telephone chair would be pushed into the center of the room, and a faint smell of sherry would hang heavily in the air. It did. Everything *was*—exactly as always. And I felt security along with anger, too—annoyed that things remained the same, relieved that my physical comforts would never change.

I moved on to my bedroom, passing one door on my left, two on my right. Colleen Sims lay in the bedroom to the left. Through the open doorway I could see her half-naked body—tall, angular, sprawled on the bed with the arms flung wide. To the right Frieda Doyle tossed in sleep. Ellen Joslin snored. They were both nervous, frustrated. They both dreamed a great deal. They both had twinges of conscience, and they were bitter enemies because, I suppose, sometimes a confirmed sinner prefers to be alone. Another sinner in the same house only points up her own sins the more. But that was a theory—not necessarily valid—only a vague idea gleaned from the long confessions of Frieda and the guarded sullenness of Ellen.

I groped on to the doorway of my own room, where I slept in a small bunk beneath the window. My roommate, Joan Crocker, was asleep, and I knew almost painful relief when I heard her rhythmical breathing. For Joan was the last person on earth I wanted to see or speak to at this moment. Tomorrow I would be questioned, condemned, confided in. Tomorrow I would hear her scorn, listen to her pleading, grit my teeth while I tried to shut out the monotonous sound of her Southern voice going on and on about the details of her intimate experiences with her husband—before he had gone overseas—before she had wandered here and stayed here and died here.

I slipped out of my clothes, pulled back the sheets of my bed, then paused, dissatisfied. Today had been planned as an escape from this house and the people in it. Yet I'd escaped nothing. Even the hat was gone, and instead of getting refreshed for a new beginning, I'd only stumbled onto another complication, a complication that I did not understand and did not like at all. I patted the sheet into place, then put a dressing robe over my nakedness and went back through the living room, out to the bluff above the sea. A few yards from the house was a wooden stairway that ran down to the beach. I sat there on the top step, the cottage behind me, the restless girls asleep, dreaming of their husbands or other men who had taken their husbands' places during the passing months. Below me was the beach, a faint white in the hazy moonlight, with the foam a brighter white along the water's edge. There was no sound, nothing to see but the winking ships out there in the darkness and a single star that hung inches above the horizon—just about, I thought, just about directly over Korea.

I smoked and did not move. I thought of my roommate who sat like this for hours at a time. Only Joan always sat on the beach in her white two-piece bathing suit. She always sat in the sunlight, and always swam nude when the other girls had left the sand in the shaded afternoon. Getting closer to Korea—naked—squelching desire or satisfying desire. Something of the sort. I sympathized with Joan, but in all those months I'd never quite understood her.

Now though, alone with only the low-hanging star and the ships that passed in the night, I came very close to understanding what went on inside the emotions of Joan Crocker. I felt myself drawn out across the black sea, out and back, as though space were being compressed and time were rushing forward or I were rushing back, moving, always moving, until suddenly a voice came to my mind, and the flat, unemotional words, *Where do we go from here?*

"Stop it!" I spoke aloud. And then very carefully, like a student searching back in history to recreate a scene long lost in time, I brought back that single day in the Presbyterian Church of Sadler Falls, New Hampshire—two years ago now—the day that had started all this, that had put me here now with my dumb eyes staring and my heart like a stone inside me....

I had not rested my head on Phil's shoulder during that late afternoon ride toward Boston. I had never felt quite so distant from him as I did then—only two hours after our marriage. And I was awed and a little frightened because he seemed to know where he was going and what he was doing all the time, though I'd never been anywhere with him before outside the county limits during his summer vacations.

"Well," he said in a matter-of-fact way. "Well, we're married."

"Yes, I guess we are."

"It takes time," he said. "I mean things have to happen, good and bad, before you're really married."

"For better or for worse," I said, and looked at his square face and knew that I'd never love anyone else as long as I lived. And I wished too that there were some way to tell my love or show my love, or simply make it felt between us.

Phil's old Chevrolet burned out some kind of wheel bearing four miles south of Portsmouth. It could not be repaired until morning, so we spent our honeymoon night in the Oak Grove Motel, where for six dollars we were given the honeymoon suite—a maple furnished living room, a bedroom, and a tile bath with shower. Phil drove into Portsmouth for champagne, and while he was gone I slipped into my new white negligee, brushed out my hair and dabbed perfume behind my ears—and then, after a second's pause, another large dab between my breasts. Phil returned and looked at me in a way that made me feel cold, and then suddenly warm all through me. He shuffled his feet, then put on a smoking jacket someone had given him. It was too large for him. The perfume hung heavy in the air. There was some difficulty opening the champagne, and when the cork finally popped, it thumped against the plaster-board ceiling, leaving a small damp spot that was still there on the following morning.

Phil said, "I feel like a damn fool in this smoking jacket." And then he looked at me in that strange way again, and he said, "Remember how you used to be ashamed of being innocent?"

"I'm not ashamed any more," I said. "I'm glad. Because of you."

I looked away from him. I stood up and went into the bedroom and pulled down the cracked green shades and turned out the overhead light, but left the fading bed-lamp burning. Then I folded back the cold sheet and slipped under the covers, sitting up with a pillow propped behind my back. I could hear Phil moving about in the other room, and I could hear my own heart pounding in my chest, and feel how much I loved him smothering me so there was only that one emotion and nothing else in the entire world. Then the light switched out and Phil's figure appeared in the doorway. He stood motionless in his shirtsleeves. He said, "I took off that damn smoking jacket."

"I thought it looked very nice," just filling the silence and trying to help ease the awkwardness.

"I felt like a fool." He came across the room and sat down on the edge of the maple bed and said, "Look, Martha, we've just been married, and I suppose it's awkward like this with everyone, and I suppose that's because all day everyone's thinking of the sex part of it, and somehow it makes it hard as hell when the time comes."

"Well," I said. "Well, I guess it does take getting used to." And then I looked away from him because I was afraid of myself—afraid of what I would say or do if I looked into his serious brown eyes for very long at a time. I laughed and said, "We don't need any blankets, I guess. I mean it's July, you know."

"No, I guess not." He slipped in bed beside me, and I lay holding my breath as he undressed me, touching only the nylon nightgown, careful that his fingers did not brush my skin.

"You smell pretty," he said. He bent forward and lightly kissed my breast. "Pretty ... I love you." And he rose suddenly and hung my negligee on a coat hanger, and even put his shoes side by side on the closet floor. Then he turned and I knew he looked at me for a long time in the dim light. I knew, even though my eyes were closed, for his own eyes seemed to warm my skin. And when I felt his weight again, beside me on the bed, and his sure hand against my body, then I thought something was sure to explode inside my chest.

The next morning was the Fourth of July. And with sleep in our eyes and the damp stain still there on the ceiling, with Phil in his undershorts and the sheets warm and rumpled, and a good breakfast ahead—suddenly then we were finally married, so that we even laughed a little during those breathless moments before getting up.

Two years ago and ages ago. And now, sitting there on the wooden steps of a cottage in Salamanca, California, with my body wrapped tightly in a red dressing robe, then suddenly the words came back—*Where do we go from here?*—and I stood abruptly and walked across the plot of ground, back through the house and down the narrow corridor to my bedroom. I took off the dressing robe, found my pajamas in the closet, and had turned toward the bed when my roommate's accusing voice spoke low behind me.

"It's late, isn't it?"

I paused, motionless. "No, I've been outside a while, I—"

"You were in San Diego a long time," Joan said.

"I know. I told you I was making a day of it."

"What did you do?"

"Well, I bought a hat."

"Is that all?"

"That's absolutely all."

"Then where's the hat?"

"Please, never mind, Joan. Please—"

"If you bought a hat, then—"

"I asked you to please never mind!" I was standing naked in the dark. I felt weary and sorry for the girl in the bed beside me. "I'm sorry, Joan." I moved close to the bed. "I didn't mean to shout." I put out a hand, touched the girl's arm, and felt a small hand move out and touch my own arm, then wing up in the dark, so that fingers brushed against my naked breast.

The fingers jerked away. "You're naked." Joan was whispering.

"I guess so. I—" I turned and went back to the bed. I slipped into pajamas, but suddenly I was cold. I pulled the covers high to my chin.

"Why are you naked?"

"I'm not." I rolled over and doubled the pillow around my head.

"Why ...? What ...? How ...? When ...?" But I did not listen. For tomorrow morning I would have to explain everything in detail. Tomorrow life would pick up exactly where it had left off. I did not want to think of tomorrow and I did not want to think of today. I wanted to think back to those days with Phil, that life with Phil ... with Phil ... with Phil! And yet there toward the end I saw another face, and there toward the end I did feel horribly naked, though I wore pajamas and was covered with a summer sheet.

CHAPTER FOUR

I HADN'T BEEN WRONG about the morning. I awoke late, and since all the other girls but Joan had left, I had to sit patiently over coffee, improvising the details of my big trip to San Diego.

Joan sat across from me at the small dinette table outside the kitchen door. A white bathing suit partially covered her thin body. Her face was pale, her brown hair disarranged, her bright eyes staring. Occasionally she shifted her slight weight on the wooden chair, and frequently she interrupted my story, pressing for the facts that I changed here and there as I went along. I did not mention the El Cortez Hotel. I knew Joan had spent her last night there with her husband. I knew their honeymoon had lasted only a week, and I did not want to bring that memory back. I did not want to start her talking.

But Joan sensed my lie all along. "You *did* go there," she insisted. "I *know* you did. You went to the El Cortez, didn't you? And I was there once too, you know. Three days, and Ned and I took a shower together, and it was kind of funny, standing there together naked under the shower. He said I was fragile. Of course I'm just bony really, but *he* said I was fragile, and that's all that counts, isn't it? What *he* says. And—and we didn't leave the room for two whole days. I bet you don't even be-believe that. But we didn't. We had our meals sent up, and then we just lay in bed and ate and—well, you've never seen Ned. He's not very handsome, I guess, and he's not very tall or heavy either. He just loves me so much that ... well...."

Her voice trailed away. She seemed embarrassed. "Don't you?" she said finally. "Don't you ever think about Phil?"

"Of course. Most all the time."

"I mean *that* way."

"I'm going to the library," I said. And I stood up quickly and went to my room to dress. I took a long time brushing my hair, making up my mouth, buttoning the sleeveless cotton dress. And I did not leave the room until Joan's weary figure appeared outside the window, slowly descending the wooden stairs to the beach below. And watching her defeated body, I felt guilty for not sticking out her story, hearing it again for the thousandth time. But the confessions of the other girls were always easier to take—variations on a theme. Joan's were always exactly the same—about her family in Louisiana and how they'd disapproved because Ned was only a marine private—how she'd met Ned at a dance in the basement of the Congregational Church while he'd been stationed at a camp near by—how they'd married in secret and had enjoyed only a week's honeymoon, three days of it spent in the El Cortez. It always ended with that same query—*Didn't I think of Phil that way?*—while the pleading haze covered her eyes until finally she went down to the beach for the hot sun bath and then the cold nude swim—the desperate attempt to erase her thoughts and the yearnings they gave her.

I pushed Joan from my mind. I gathered my library books and automatically planned my day. A trip to the library, coffee, perhaps a swim later on. I would write Phil, read a novel. I would listen to my housemates' fights and confessions, and I would keep my mind carefully balanced at all times. I would never think of yesterday again.

The library came first. I tucked the books under my arm and went out into the early sun and through the streets, past the empty swimming pool and along the gravel drive by the main house. Our landlord, Lloyd Watkins, was standing in a window as I passed. He wore a black dressing robe over his pajamas. His close-cropped hair was blond above his tanned face, and his tall body was bent slightly forward behind the glass, strong and boyish for a man in his early forties. I hesitated, then waved a good morning. But his hands remained stiff in the pockets of his robe. I could feel his eyes watching me though I hurried on down the drive and past the decorative columns. I did not walk slowly again until I'd reached the street.

Once in the residential section, I shifted the library novels under my other arm and dropped my cigarette to the sidewalk, thinking that my squeamishness about smoking on the street was a little silly really, an unwanted vestige of my New England background. Then I moved on through the town, keeping on the shaded side of the street because though a California sun is fine on the beach, it's miserable through even the thinnest cotton dress. Before me was the concrete bridge that spans the highway between San Diego twelve miles to the south and Los Angeles some hundred miles to the north. Behind me were the low, modern homes of Salamanca's younger wealthy set, and behind that the ever-present sea, which by its very calm gave every wife in town the illusion that just beyond its rim, a few yards beyond that destroyer's funnel, was that strange land called Korea, where her particular husband was the number one priority target for the Communist high command. I crossed the highway and entered the town itself, white and nearly gay in the morning sun, with its smart shops displaying beach clothes, alligator bags, television sets, and those bar accessories that cocktail drinkers like to buy, use once, and then forsake for can openers, hammers, and kitchen ice picks.

Red-faced marines from Camp Pendleton lounged about on corners or bounced from cafes or strode side by side, forcing others to step down to the gutter; naval officers sauntered by with their shoulders stiff and their gold stripes bright in the sun; and sailors wandered about in their own aimless ways, ready to go anywhere or do anything, but frustrated because somehow their very eagerness had made them lose direction. And there were women, many of them, mostly young, wearing gold wedding bands and slacks and gay cotton blouses, moving with the lethargy of the sailors, taking the admiring whistles with a smile or a slowing or hastening of their walk—or sometimes with that cold indifference which marks women who have neither an imagination nor a sense of humor.

The library was on the far side of town. The librarian was a gray-haired spinster who disapproved of the wives who invaded her sanctum and often kept her books long overdue. She nodded at me, demanded my twelve-cent fine like a judge demanding payment in a drunken driving case. I selected three new novels and left, only nodding a quick goodbye.

The sun was high now, hot on my face. At the local tea shop I paused and looked through the window at the familiar faces of the women who collected there every morning at this time—and often stayed there throughout the remainder of the day. I did not want to go in, but entered all the same. I did not want coffee, but ordered it all the same. And while I waited, I listened to the talk around me.

"Nothing below a commander, my eye! I know a sailor boy who picked her up on a Saturday night and couldn't get rid of her till three o'clock Sunday afternoon." That was the first clear sentence I heard. But it did not startle me, did not shock me. For I'd heard many voices, many words, many ideas like that in the past few months.

I looked absently into my coffee cup, then turned my head and recognized the accusing girl as a casual friend. I nodded, and she leaned toward me. She was that indeterminate young-wife-age of all the wives in Salamanca, and her green eyes were bright with false amusement.

"You know," she said. "You know, Martha, I just figured it out. We sit too much. We think too much." It was a brilliant idea. She straightened and looked about at the other girls packed tightly into the tea room. "We sit too much. That's the trouble." Then, as an after-thought, she added, "Or lie down too much." And she giggled, then let the giggle drop to a mock whine. "But Martha doesn't have any complaints. Not where she's living. And I know, because I've been at parties in the main house. All glass and brick and—"

"Yes, it's nice and I'm lucky." I finished my coffee, then stood, feeling a touch of irritation as I stuffed cigarettes into my straw purse, tucked my library books under a bare arm, and walked back toward the doorway. But there was nowhere to go really, except back to Joan, back to the long, long thoughts. I paused, then sat once more at a small table near the doorway. I looked out the window at the street, bathed now in the afternoon light of a California sun. I listened to the women's voices rising in the smoky air around me, going on and on, about clothes, about men, about yesterday and this afternoon and tomorrow, always avoiding what was uppermost in all their minds, lying there so big that it could not be expressed, seldom mentioned, and only thought of in a detached, almost wondering way. When would their husbands return?

The coffee was gone. The morning had passed. I stood, left a quarter on the small table, and turned into the room, pulling the library books against my side. Still the voices went on around me, punctuated with the laughter of false gaiety, making complaints and accusations and just plain talk for its own sake—to fill in that numb void left by the kind of loneliness that only one person on earth can ever really fill. I glanced over the familiar and half-familiar faces, and again, as I had frequently now in the past weeks, I saw quite clearly through the flashing eyes and the tanned skins and the desperate smiles. I saw these women for what they had become.

And I heard their deadly voices: "Of course I didn't sleep with him, because after all, he's shipping out on Tuesday, and there's no point in getting involved in something you can't play with and nurse along over a period of time.... I've been working on a tan for six hours a day, but then it always flakes off right when it gets the best.... Me, I go to the movies every afternoon, so I won't have to live between those miserable hours of one to four.... Did you know her husband was killed on Heartbreak Ridge?" And other voices saying, "I slapped his face.... I'll never speak to her again.... She borrowed my best skirt and of course she hasn't returned it."

Someone spoke my name. "Martha, did you hear about that new girl over at—"

"I heard she's been sleeping with—" Then I stopped, turned slowly, and looked at the girl's face. I walked quickly toward the door. Somewhere, through the smoke, I had suddenly seen my own image sitting there among them all, different only in what I thought and how I acted within a space that grew smaller with each passing day.

"That's what I want to know. Who's the man she's—"

But I went on through the doorway, leaving the voice and the faces—and the image of myself—behind in the smoke-filled room.

It was hot in the noonday sun. Perspiration formed on my forehead, rolled in drops down my face. My clothes were damp. They clung to my body. I moved slowly, getting through the day, getting through the day. A sailor went by, winking. A marine said the same old words, the same old *Going somewhere? Going somewhere? Going somewhere? Going somewhere?* The same old words went over and over in the heat as I moved along.

"Going somewhere?" But this time a rough hand touched my arm. I started and swung my eyes to the red face of a navy commander. He was confident. He leered at me. He acted as though we knew each other from other times and other places. Where was it? Some train? Some party? Well, the hell with it! The point was the heat and how fine a drink would go. And after that ... well ... after that ... and he talked on. I pulled my arm back gently, but his fingers closed even more firmly about my wrist.

"Look," I said. And then seeing the purpose in his eyes, "Please—listen—"

"All the same," he muttered. "You're all the same."

"So are you bastards!" The low voice came from a jeep alongside the curb. Then another officer appeared, a lieutenant this time. He was tall with a hooked nose. His mouth was clamped shut, his eyes closed to points. "On your way," he said. "On your way, sailor!" It was Hank McKellar.

The commander said something about rank, and Hank laughed, but his lips did not move. The commander's face puffed into a bright red. "A whore," he said. "For Christ's sake, all this over a lousy—"

He did not finish. I watched and could not move. My breath was stopped inside my chest, my eyes glued on the thin line of Hank's mouth and the fist that flashed from nowhere and landed with a sharp crack on the commander's face. Hank hit the man again and again—three or four times in the face, once in the stomach. There was bright red on the commander's mouth. It dripped from his nose and ran along his chin. He started to crumble, but Hank held him up by the coat lapel, then knocked him to the sidewalk. He picked him up again and slammed his head back against the brick side of the building. All the time he was muttering under his breath,

"You bastard … you stinking bastard … every one of you … every God damn one of you!" until finally he stopped, panting, still muttering, almost crying with his anger. Then he jerked around and stared at the small crowd that had gathered around us. They were mostly sailors. They were grinning, enjoying themselves.

Hank swore. He grabbed my arm, forced his way through the crowd, and pulled me down the small alley beside the building. He pushed open the rear door of a haberdashery, led me through and out to another street a block from where the fight had occurred. Another doorway, another alley, and then another. I moved blindly behind him, wincing at the pain of his fingers that clutched my arm. Blood was on his knuckles. It flowed onto the brown skin of my bare arm, and when we finally stopped in the last alley of all, panting in the sun among a litter of garbage cans behind a grocery store, the blood had dribbled down my arm so that I felt it on my fingers and in the palm of my hand.

Hank let go. I was leaning back against a locked door in an abandoned doorway. It was hotter than ever. My clothes were soaked with perspiration. My mind was still focused on Hank's fist and his crazy anger—on the commander's blood-spattered face and the trickle of Hank's blood on my own bare arm.

"The son-of-a-bitch!" Hank said.

I shifted the books that I'd held all this time. "You didn't have to go crazy—as if you hated everyone—as if you could kill him."

"I didn't go to Annapolis. Some of those bastards won't give you a chance. To hell with them! Finish what you start, they tell you. Do your duty. So from now on I finish what I start. You laughed at me for saying that once. On the ship. College boy stuff.

Calculated risk. You laughed." He was talking in short, blunt sentences. full of hatred and resentment.

"Hank—" I pulled my eyes to his face. It was glistening with sweat. His voice died away and I watched his eyes drop slowly down along my own face and neck, down to my dress. Then I felt the hard pressure of my own breasts against the cotton, and the outline of that tautness showed through the damp cloth in painful detail. I knew Hank watched but there was nothing I could do.

"Nothing to worry about." His eyes were still on my dress. "Those sailors won't talk. They loved it. And the commander won't talk, so ..." His voice trailed off, then came back again, softly now. "I was looking for you. Called at the cottage ... looking for you...." He wet his lips and put his knuckles to his mouth, and I could almost taste the blood. "Why are you like that?" his eyes still on my clinging dress. "The blood? Does fighting excite you? Why are you ...?"

He moved closer and dizziness came so that I could scarcely see his face at all. My fingernails were dug hard into my palms, and when I was sure my body would burst in the intense heat of the day and the fierce burning of his eyes, I pulled sharply from the doorway, stumbled through the rubbish of the alley, and ran crazily out to the street. People were passing, staring at me with wonder and amusement. Behind me Hank's voice called out sharply. I turned into the nearest doorway, a theatre with the girl lolling in the booth. It was a girl I knew, one of the luckier wives who'd found a job. "Pay you later," I panted, and I stumbled on into the darkened theatre, down the side aisle to a seat against the wall.

I closed my eyes and waited.

CHAPTER FIVE

THE MOVIE was a third over, but it did not matter. I kept my eyes closed, and recognized the voice of Randolph Scott, and heard the firing of guns and the clop of horses' hoofs. After a few moments I felt the chill of the air-conditioning system against my body. The perspiration dried on my face. My clothes no longer stuck, and I breathed more easily, relaxed in the dark and the cooling air. And after my heart had completely stopped its pounding, I went into the powder room, washed my dirt-streaked face, brushed my hair, and carefully wiped the dried blood from my arm. I was hungry, so I bought popcorn in the lobby. The picture had ended then. A newsreel came on, and I stood at the rear of the theatre, eating the popcorn, watching the shells burst on the hillsides of some Korean mountain, watching the wounded carried limp down the rocky slope, placed into helicopters, flown out to the nearest hospital. The announcer said that all wounded received the best of medical care. Then the picture changed to a conference building, and another announcer said the peace talks had bogged down again.

"Everything is bogged down." I spoke aloud. My own voice surprised me, and I turned and went back through the lobby, feeling oddly relaxed now that I'd seen those war films, now that Phil had returned to reality, though perhaps on one of those stretchers, and perhaps in one of those ditches along the road.

I paid the girl in the ticket booth, then walked back through the town in the shadowed afternoon. Hank's jeep was no longer beside the curb. But splotches of blood were still visible, dried hard and black, on the sidewalk. I stared at them absently, then bent and picked up a small shiny object—the two silver bars of a naval lieutenant's uniform. I slipped the bars in my purse, thinking to return them to Hank, and then remembered as I moved on through the town, that of course, of course—of course, *of course*—I would never see Hank McKellar again. I took the insignia from my purse and dropped it into the gutter. A small boy picked it up immediately. I started to call after him that it was mine, that I'd dropped it by mistake. Then I changed my mind and walked on through the quiet streets, concentrating on the faces of the people whom I passed, finding them new, welcomed, almost refreshing.

At the highway I crossed the street into the shade and paused as a high voice sounded behind me. "Hey, Martha!" The click of new heels grew louder, and I turned and watched the girl move toward me from under the green and white striped awning of the Corsair Hotel. It was Frieda Doyle, the most adventurous of my four housemates. She was a slender thing, childlike, with large violet eyes and bright red hair, with a firm small body—narrow hips and breasts that tilted upward like the breasts of caricatured women in French cartoons. She was panting when she reached my side. "Going back? Been to the library?" with her orange-red lips moist in the sunlight. "Wish I could read." She laughed and swung into step. "But books always make me envy people in them."

I laughed with her, thinking, yes, I'd been to the library. I really had, though it seemed ages ago. "You were in the Corsair?" I asked.

"That j.g. The blond one with those funny eyes. But I walked out on him."

When we'd reached the residential section, we walked slowly beneath the huge trees, past the big homes that faced the sea. As we turned up Lloyd's driveway, we saw a green Jaguar convertible parked under the low portico. "That means he's home," Frieda murmured.

"Who?"

"Lloyd, of course." She screwed up her soft eyes. "Who else?"

"All right," I said. "All right, Frieda." I turned away, not wanting to hear now, on this wearing afternoon, what I already knew—that Lloyd Watkins had what Frieda called "an eye for me." I'd known that from the moment I'd met Lloyd a month or so after my arrival in Salamanca, when I'd gone to a party in his big glass-brick house, when a young wife had danced nearly naked on his dining-room table, and he'd kept his eyes on me all the time before saying, "There's only four girls in my guest house and the rent's free and there's room for one more."

I'd accepted the invitation because I'd been living alone in a rooming house, and four housemates promised protection against any ideas Lloyd Watkins might have had in mind. Still Lloyd had kept that "eye for me" during the months I'd lived on his property. I'd become more conscious of it every day, feeling a twinge of awkwardness under his unblinking gaze each time he mentally undressed me. I'd even wondered whether or not his piercing eyes could see the tiny mole on my left side or the scar where my appendix had been removed. And despite it all, despite Lloyd's open affair with our housemate, Ellen Joslin, I still felt he was not really interested in women at all.

I knew all about Mr. Lloyd Watkins. I said, "Come on, Frieda."

But she hesitated, listening. "He's playing his jazz records."

"So?"

"I don't know a better time to beg a good martini. If Ellen's not with him. God, that Ellen!" She turned away, and her slim body moved on up the gravel drive toward the big house with the sun making patterns on the windows.

I walked on toward the guest house, through the unpruned trees, until I reached the empty swimming pool. I paused, then sat on the pool's edge, trying hopelessly to forget this day, trying to succumb to the quiet peace of late afternoon, and succumbing against my will to the unrest I always felt after being with Frieda Doyle. Frieda was one of those rare girls who never pay the consequences for their wrong doings. She had married a naval flier and lived with him only a few months before he went off on a carrier and she became one of us five wives in "the girl cage," as envious other wives liked to call our adobe house. And since her first day here, Frieda had had one amusing affair after another. *Amusing* is the correct word too, because none of Freida's affairs were serious, and she never lost her love for her own husband. It was a paradox I found difficult to understand, except through the wandering explanations Frieda had given me herself. For one thing, she never gave herself to a man. She was always careful to be taken, always careful to show little if any passion, and always amused by the passion of the man who took her.

The point about Frieda was that she kept her body quite separate from her mind and emotions. Her thoughts, her love, her very passion was directed at no one but her husband. If her lovely body gave someone else pleasure, no other part of her being went with it.

But I did not want to think about Frieda Doyle. I did not like to suspect that moral values were not the same in Salamanca as they were in Sadler Falls, not the same with Frieda as they were with me. Or perhaps it was a matter of desires instead of values—and perhaps my desires were becoming more like Frieda's every day.

I shook my head, then stood abruptly and walked on through the trees, across the small clearing to the adobe guest house. I stood quietly, looking down at the small beach that lay cupped between high rocks at either end of the cove. Now in the late afternoon, the last of the guests were leaving the sand. Only Joan Crocker remained, thin, standing firm in her white two-piece bathing suit. Poor Joan, nervous, frustrated, terribly in love and always terribly alone. I watched her a moment, feeling compassion for her as always, waiting for what I knew would come when the last visitor had disappeared down the beach. I watched, and in the last sun of afternoon, I saw the ritual performed again for the hundredth time. First she glanced furtively about. She pulled on her bathing cap, tested the water with her toe, then edged out farther toward Korea. She stood motionless, then plunged into the water, and reappeared a moment later, her shoulders white above the sea, the parts of her bathing suit held tight in either hand.

I turned abruptly and walked into the house. I went to my room, sat on my bed, opened a book, read a few lines, and put the book down again. I decided to write a letter to Phil, changed my mind, and read his last one for the second time. It was the same as every other letter. He was getting along all right. He hoped I was fine, and he was getting along all right. Finally I stood and moved out to the living room. It was small but comfortable, and oppressively silent since my four housemates were all busy with their personal interests.

But Joan came up from the beach a moment later. Her nervous fingers played with the doorframe, the lamps, the ashtrays, anything that came within reach. One hand clutched her white beach robe about her thin shoulders. "No mail," she murmured.

"I didn't get any mail. It's been a long time and no mail...." And she continued on to our bedroom.

Then, gradually, the other girls appeared. Frieda back from Lloyd's, where she'd had one cocktail before leaving under Ellen Joslin's jealous eyes. According to Frieda, she'd walked in without knocking and found Ellen posing for Lloyd, her dress pulled down to her waist.

But Ellen came in at that very moment. Her full body tensed. Her black eyes blazed. "You bitch! You bitch!" while Frieda laughed and I came between them as I'd done before, many times before, in the past long months.

Joan was there, dressed now, disapproving as always, her eyes vacant, her words always mumbled beneath her breath. And finally Colleen Sims appeared, so that we were all together now. Colleen, though, was at least cheerful. She'd been to the naval hospital where she went three days a week to entertain the wounded. And even now she could sit, relaxed, her long legs crossed, her body hunched forward, and strum that guitar as though we were all just five happy little girls on a college henparty.

Darkness came. We ate. We argued. Frieda changed her clothes and went out on some tentative date. Everything kept going according to schedule. Joan fretted and Ellen pouted and Colleen strummed absently on her guitar. Everything according to schedule, except the restlessness within me. Because somehow now, after today and yesterday, I could not become interested in the lifesaving details that had meant so much in the past. I tried to read, but could not get past the first twenty pages. I walked on a darkened beach and caught myself running as though trying to escape some ominous shape that was always there behind me. And safe in the cottage, lying in my bed with the moon outside the window and the clock ticking monotonously on the dresser, I knew that tonight I would not sleep until the drug of extreme weariness overcame me. It was the first time I'd felt this way since Phil had left, and I knew that for the moment there was nothing I could do about it.

So I was still awake, still staring into the darkness, listening to the ticking clock when the telephone rang sharply from the living room. I heard it as something apart, unreal, unwanted— yet all that I had lain awake for during this entire night.

Joan sat up in bed, whispering, "I dreamed about it. Ned, you see. He was killed and somebody's calling me, and—"

"For Frieda probably." I said it casually, but tried to keep from running as I moved painfully toward the living room. I lifted the receiver, said, "Yes?" and finally felt relaxed, almost at ease, as I heard the remembered voice.

"You ran out on me."

"Yes...." finding nothing more to say.

"I'm in a bar." And a pause and, "I'm buying drinks for all beautiful blondes named Martha."

"It's terribly late."

"And you were in bed, and now you're sitting in your pajamas."

I laughed a little and noticed my pajama jacket was not properly buttoned. I noticed too that there was silence on the phone, as though his gray eyes were watching me. I shivered and buttoned the jacket to my neck and said, "I don't think you ought to telephone."

"I ought to see you. Tomorrow night."

"No...."

"I'll be around tomorrow night."

"I won't be here. I simply won't be here!"

"Then why don't you hang up? Why did you answer the phone?"

"I didn't know who it was."

"You knew."

My fingers tightened on the cord. I forced them to relax, and ran my tongue over my lips. Hank was still talking whem I hung up slowly and stood and walked dumbly back to my room.

Joan was sitting upright in bed. She said, "It wasn't for Frieda."

"No."

"It was for you."

"An old friend. Someone I know." I slipped into bed and lay there motionless, hearing Joan's voice go on, saying, "You're not fooling me. Oh, you've tried to, all right. But you're just like the rest of them around this town. You get bored, and you meet some man and forget all about your husband...." On and on, while I struggled for sleep, and the words became mixed and straightened out again, so that finally I saw them all before me—all these wives on the West Coast—crawling aimlessly like ants on a golden hill. Scores of wives—wives who could not work, did not want to work, and probably couldn't have found work if they'd tried—wives who'd given up their homes in order to live close to a husband's base or home port, and were using their bottled-up energies in a fierce resistance or a fierce acceptance of other men. Formerly contented housewives, who now were not quite certain whether or not they were wives at all, yet clung with slipping fingers to the fact that they were still women, not getting any younger, but becoming more frustrated, more lonely and more achingly bored with each passing day.

"I won't be here." I was talking aloud. "I told you I won't be here!"

Far away a ship's whistle sounded in the dark.

CHAPTER SIX

Somehow I could not get Hank McKellar from my mind, even though I'd sworn not to see him again. I was not at all sure I liked him, and saw no reason why he should frighten or anger me any more than any of the other men I'd met here and there around the town. I told myself that I was dramatizing everything these days. Hank was the first man I'd had any personal connection with since my marriage. So it was only natural for him to stick in my mind after a trip to San Diego, a street fight in broad daylight, an early morning phone call. Yet it was not the evening in San Diego, any more than it was the fight or the phone call, as such, that disturbed me most. Rather it was the little things, the pieces of those times that I remembered most vividly—the way I'd pulled away when he'd touched the hat's veil that time on the ship; his khakis hanging in the stateroom locker; the anger when I'd laughed at him; his fist smashing the commander's face; his eyes on me; and the way I'd felt naked while talking to him on the phone, afraid that he could see me from the other end of the wire.

Actually I could not remember Hank himself in any detail. His nose was slightly hooked. I remembered that. His eyes were frightening until he smiled. His hands were strong, with long unmanicured nails. He was not handsome, and I knew nothing about him at all as a person, except that he was fighting the world single-handed, and fighting something he did not like within himself. He was a stranger who'd gotten under my skin. He was a strange man who might eventually make some difference to me, if I did not stop it fast, with no concern for him, and no sympathy for myself.

So when Frieda asked me to chaperone her with a new-found army major to the Beach Club that night, I remembered Hank's promise to call and my own promise that I would not be there. "I'll go," I told Frieda. "I'd love to go."

"I've met this major once," Frieda explained coyly, "and I told him I was brought up very properly, and always had a chaperone on my first date. I guess it does sound silly. But really, Martha, I'm turning over a new leaf. I really am. So if you'll come along with me, you see, then he won't get any ideas. Or rather he'll know his ideas won't work right away, and of course I won't get any ideas either, so ..."

"So I'm supposed to protect you against yourself?"

"Well, not exactly." There was something ingenuous in the way she lowered her eyes. Something almost childish.

"Just joking," I said. "And I'd really like to go," though I did not tell her that in my own way, I too was asking to be protected from myself.

Frieda's major arrived about eight. He was a rough, leather-faced man in his late forties. His name was Major Kermit Mullins, a name that kept slipping Frieda's mind, so that she continually called him "Major," which seemed to irritate him a good deal. I irritated him too. He didn't understand why Frieda should need a chaperone.

"Because," Frieda explained, "because I *am* married, you know."

There was nothing the major could say, and all the way down to the Beach Club he sat in a corner of the cab, grumbling, beginning to feel sure that he'd made a bad mistake in picking Frieda up at all on that day or so before.

The Salamanca Beach Club was private only in that it charged a dollar and a half for a middle-priced whisky. Now in the second summer of the Korean war, most of the customers were marine and naval officers from San Diego, who'd saved cash because they'd been where they couldn't spend it, found restless wives who could help alleviate the problem, and were determined to get their money's worth. The major headed straight for the bar, climbed onto a red plastic-topped stool, pulled one up beside him for Frieda, and ordered three double scotches. He took a long drink, stared at the nude in the reproduction of Benton's "Persephone" over the bar, and said, "Well, here we are; well, here we are"

I perched on a stool beside Frieda. I looked at my own face in the glass. It seemed haunted, frightened, like the face of a criminal on a post office bulletin board. Frieda and the major were talking nonsense, and I realized then that my chaperoning duties would end abruptly after the very first drink. So I had another and then another. I felt them immediately. I was hungry. A small orchestra was playing in the dining room, and the music scraped somewhere inside my head. A marine lieutenant wandered by, winking suggestively. He leaned on the bar, looked down the front of my dress.

I was getting tight for the first time since Phil hadn't been around to put me to bed and make fun of me in the morning when we both had hangovers. Yes, I was getting tight, thinking of a lean man and not a square man, thinking of gray eyes and not brown eyes, getting mixed up and getting tight, of course. Of course getting tight.

I stood, leaned against the table, excused myself, then headed off toward the powder room. I was seated in a leatherette chair, making up my mouth, trying to convince myself that such mixed-up thoughts were only natural when one was tight, when

Frieda burst in through the swinging door. She was smiling her innocent smile, saying, "I thought you were protecting me."

"I am, Frieda. Oh, yes, I am."

"He's not so bad, really." Frieda made up her pouting lips, drawing them thick and moist. She caught my eye in the mirror. "I mean he's very nice, really. I mean—"

"I know what you mean," I said.

"Well, what I mean is if he takes me home alone, will you be all right? I mean he's already got the idea it's hands off, so it's quite safe for him to take me home alone, and I wouldn't want him to think I'm a *prig*. I mean being nice is one thing, but a *prig!*"

"Don't worry," I said. "You're not a prig, Frieda. And I'll fight anyone who says you are." I glanced up at Frieda's smiling face, nodded, heard her say, "You're sweet, darling," and watched her move out through the doorway. I wondered if Hank had called at the guest house. I wondered why I cared. And I wondered idly how it felt to be carefree like Frieda Doyle.

Frieda and the major were gone when I returned to the bar. But Lloyd Watkins was sitting alone at a corner table, his handsome face silhouetted against the windows, one finger tapping up and down on the red plastic. I paused, remembering Ellen's intense jealousy of anyone who spoke to Lloyd. I turned and slipped back through the doorway and walked absently across the lobby.

An army captain came by and said, "You ditched, baby?"

"No," not looking at him.

"Want a drink? Want to comfort a little old soldier who's shipping out tomorrow?"

But I did not answer. I moved on through the lobby, where a radio was playing, an announcer's voice repeating the same discouraging news about how the Korean peace talks had bogged down again. My head was still spinning from the drinks. I pushed open the glass door, went out to the cooling night, and stood motionless in the doorway, letting the cool air blow across my face. And when the voice sounded low behind me, I started, bracing myself on the doorframe.

"Where was it? The El Cortez? Some alley somewhere?" Hank stood close. His breath touched the back of my neck. I dug my fingers into the doorframe, and my voice sounded odd as I said the first thing that entered my head. "How did you know—"

"I'm very bright. I ask questions."

"I thought I told you—"

"You told me."

"Well—And I felt let-down, as though I'd been waiting for this moment all along.

"You need coffee," he said.

"I guess so. I'm a little tight, I guess. I don't know why. It's been a long time. I don't know what's the matter with me."

"Don't you?"

"No, I don't." And I said it again. "No, I don't," as he guided me across the gravel drive to his waiting jeep.

We drank coffee in a drug store. It was white and clean, with fluorescent lights, and quarter-cut custard pies under gleaming glass along the counter. Hank said nothing the whole time, but I could feel his eyes watching me in the spaces of mirror between the coffee urns. I kept my own eyes on my coffee. I drummed my fingers on the marble counter. I smoked, and moved my spoon around and around in the brown liquid. "I told you on the phone," I said finally. "As far as you're concerned, I'm not around any more. I'm out. I've gone away."

"You love this guy Phil?"

"You asked me that before."

"I'm asking again."

"I told you before."

"I just like to hear you say it. I keep hoping it will make me change my mind about a couple of things." He slipped off the stool and strode ahead of me out to the night and the jeep at the curb. "I'll take you home," he said grimly. "I won't bother you any more." And then, when I did not answer, he said, "But it's not that easy. In fact it's difficult as hell." And he took my elbow and helped me into the jeep. Then he climbed in himself and started the engine and said, "Fresh air. That's it. Fresh air." He swung the car onto the highway and drove fast through town so the cool air blew against our faces. The light was red before the Corsair. The jeep's motor idled unsteadily, and Hank's head turned and looked beyond me toward the lighted hotel. "Want to go in for a crème de menthe? Saw it in a movie once. Lady felt lousy, so she had a crème de menthe."

"No thank you." I looked absently at the entrance to the hotel, saw a cab stop in front, saw Frieda climb out on the arm of her Major Mullins and walk beside him into the lobby. Then the light turned green and we raced on down the highway. "Goodbye," I murmured. "Goodbye, Frieda."

"Who?"

"Goodbye, Martha."

"Hank," he said. "Hank McKellar. And you've told me good-bye before."

The jeep raced on down the highway. I looked for words, finally said his name for no reason at all. "Hank McKellar ... Hank McKellar."

"Martha Gwynn," he said.

"No, I ... I just wanted to make sure I remember your name."

"Does it make a difference?"

"No, but I ..." And I was silent, thinking of Frieda again. I moved closer to the side, my body tense on the tiny seat. It seemed that Hank was laughing, except that there was no sound but the tires on the pavement. His officer's hat was pushed to the back of his head, and his face was a jagged profile cut hastily from black cardboard. He brought the jeep to a stop, swung hard on the wheel, and a second later we were bouncing down a gravel road toward the beach. I held onto the sides, and I told myself, "This is it. This is the end right here. We park and he makes a pass at me and gets mad when I don't give in. But finally he says to hell with it and drives me back to the guest house. He gets sullen because Hank McKellar never starts what he can't finish. Except this time, because here's something even Hank McKellar can't finish." The certainty of what would happen gave me a sense of peculiar relief. Yet there was a numb sadness inside me as the little car dropped down until we were on the beach itself, riding along the sand of the cove.

"Quite a little car," Hank said after a long time. "Quite a little girl." He drove faster, turning suddenly, backing up, then driving recklessly with two wheels in the sea so the water splashed out on either side of us.

I held onto the seat and told myself to let him blow off steam, let him get it all out of himself. But there was no sense in the way he was acting. He was laughing, saying, "I'm taking you for a ride, baby. You understand? I'm taking you for a ride." Then the laughter stopped. It hung there in the night for a long time before it was gone into the surf. "I'm in love with you." He said it flatly as if he hated every word of it. "I love you and I want you—and that's the way it goes."

There was nothing to say. I sat there, limp, confused, wanting him, too, yet strangely unhappy because of that answering need for him that nagged at my insides.

Suddenly his arm slid around me and he pulled me against him. His face came toward mine and I saw the intense, agonized expression in his eyes, the taut, hungry lines of his mouth. Then that mouth was hot against mine and I felt as if I were being sucked into him. The kiss went on and on and I knew I didn't want it to end. He was hurting me but I no longer cared.

"Martha!" he said hoarsely. "You've got to." He tried to pull me closer and his fingers began to fumble with the neck of my dress.

"No, Hank. Not now." The hoarseness of my voice matched his own. I pushed his hand away. But it was a distinct effort. I knew if he insisted I wouldn't be able to stop him—I would no longer want to stop him.

For a long moment he was rigid and still. I could feel the blood pounding in my body. I saw the way Hank was trembling. I saw the pain in his eyes. Then he buried his lips in my hair and his hands scraped harshly up and down my back.

"All right." His voice was that of a stranger. "I'll drive you home. And then I'm getting the hell back to San Diego and try not to think about you again."

"I'm sorry, Hank," I whispered, my hands clasped tightly in my lap. I tried to smile but I was crying inside, crying like a lost child.

He didn't say anything. Instead, he started the engine, swung the jeep around hard in the sand.

CHAPTER SEVEN

AWOKE EARLY, ate breakfast alone, then returned to my room. I waited until Joan had gone to the beach, then started a letter to Phil, telling him I was perfectly all right and my four housemates were wonderful company. But somehow I could not seem to end the letter. I stuffed my rumpled clothes into the laundry bag, trying to get rid of every physical reminder of Hank McKellar.

Frieda came in, dressed in pajamas, her eyes filled with sleep. She held a coffee cup in a trembling hand. She sat on Joan's bed and laughed. "God, oh, God!"

I smiled weakly, still struggling with the end of that letter to Phil. "Last night," I wrote, "I went to the Beach Club with Frieda Doyle and an old friend of hers from the army. Not much fun without you, but it was good to get out of the cottage for a change, although I did go to San Diego two days ago. But nothing very interesting happened then either...."

"You know what happened?" Frieda was going to become confidential.

I said, "What?" and made small doodling marks on the side of the paper while Frieda laughed and squirmed and gave me all the details.

It seemed that after she'd left me in the powder room of the Beach Club, she'd returned to the bar and sat down on the stool and said, "How about another drink?"

Then the major had said, "I've got some very good stuff in my room," and she hadn't seen much harm in an innocent drink, so they'd stood up, and Frieda had shrugged and walked beside the major out through the bar and down to the gravel parking lot. "I'll get a cab," he'd said, and he'd touched her arm, started to kiss her, then changed his mind and said, "You're married, aren't you?"

She'd been irritated. She'd said, "I've already told you, haven't I? His name is Harry, and I married him a year ago in Las Vegas. He's a navy flier and a terrific guy."

A cab had swung into the drive and the major had hailed it and opened the door. Once inside he'd lighted a cigarette and sat carefully in his own corner. Frieda had watched him. She'd decided that except for his thinning hair he was very good-looking really, in a ruddy sort of way, and she'd wondered if he were married himself, but had decided not to ask.

They'd had a drink in the bar of the Corsair. The major had repeated that he had a bottle of very good stuff in his room, so they'd gone up in the elevator and the major had taken off his coat and loosened his tie. He'd ordered ice and gotten a pitcher of water from the bathroom.

All the time Frieda had walked back and forth in the room, conscious of the major's eyes on her legs and back and the way her breasts moved beneath her dress. She'd paused before his tan leather bag, studied the gold initials, *KM*, and wondered why his name kept slipping her mind.

Then the bellhop had arrived with ice. He was an old, wizened man, who had eyed her and might have smiled a little. She'd reminded herself never to come to the Corsair again with anybody because the bellboys always remembered and instead of nodding or speaking, they just pretended they'd never seen the woman before, and that made it all the worse.

The major had poured their drinks and they'd sat on the edge of his bed, and the major had said, "You don't look as though you had any bones at all."

But Frieda had not answered. She'd smoothed down her skirt, swallowed her drink, stood and poured another. The major's face had been hazy when she'd returned to the bed, and when he'd put an arm over her shoulders, she'd pretended not to feel the pressure. When he'd pulled her down beside him she'd thought only that I had deserted her in her hour of need. And then, when his hands had found her, she'd caught herself saying, "Please, Kermit!" and remembering then that his name was Kermit Mullins, so that everything had been all right really.

"But I'm not going up to that hotel again." She stood then and moved closer to where I sat behind the tiny table, still doodling on the paper. "You're not mad at me, are you, Martha?"

"No."

"After all, you got sort of tight, so you didn't chaperone me and—"

"Let's not be silly, Frieda."

"Well, I told you I'm not going up there again." She started for the door. I looked at my doodling marks and saw that I'd drawn a naval lieutenant's silver bars. I scratched it out hurriedly, then turned and said, "Frieda, tell me something. Why do you do it?"

"What?"

"Just—well, sleep with men like that? Men you don't even know?"

"I know Kermit. I told you I met him before, and—"

"But why do you do it?"

For a second she did not answer. She just stood there in her blue pajamas, her eyes frowning, her red hair rumpled about her head. "Why?" she said. And then she shrugged. "Because it's fun, I guess—because I—well, I like to." It was an honest answer. She laughed and walked out of the room.

For a long time I did not move. I stared at the letter I had written, and somehow it looked false. Colleen Sims pushed her head in the doorway and said, "Good morning." Then, a moment later, I heard her guitar strumming in the living room. I picked up the letter and tore it very carefully into tiny pieces, and was dropping the pieces into the wastebasket one by one when the angry voices echoed out from the living room.

"So Lloyd doesn't want you any more!" That was Frieda. "He was alone at the Beach Club last night, and if that doesn't prove it, then—" And Ellen's voice interrupted, calling Frieda a whore while Frieda screamed back until their voices mingled into one rising screech. Something crashed, and I heard the splintered pieces of china scattering about on the floor. Then I rose and walked out to the living room. I did not run because Ellen and Frieda had fought before, and for a moment I only stood in the doorway watching, feeling nothing but a deep weariness.

Their screaming had turned to violence. They were tearing at each other's clothes, pulling each other's hair. Ellen wore a yellow robe that was ripped from her shoulders, and Frieda's pajama top was torn and fell away completely, until in a moment they were two squirming, half-naked bodies rolling over and over on the living room floor. Then suddenly it was over. Frieda lay flat on her back with Ellen sitting astride her stomach, holding Frieda's arms wide. Perspiration ran down Ellen's heaving naked back. She started to slap Frieda's face, then changed her mind, stood up and said, "What's the use? What the hell is the use?" and moved slowly down to her room.

Frieda lay motionless, naked except for her torn pajama bottom that barely covered her childlike thighs. Her pink-tipped breasts quivered as she panted. Her eyes were closed, her red hair disarranged. "The bitch!" she said.

"Are you all right, Frieda?"

"The bitch!"

"She's all right." Colleen had not moved during the entire struggle. She sat behind the dinette table, sipping coffee, strumming absently on her guitar. "Just a routine matter settled in a routine way."

"I guess so," I said. I went back to my room, locked the door, and tried again and again to write that letter to Phil. In the end I did compose a short note. And in the end I realized that from now on all my future letters would be like this one—short because each day I left out more, and padded now and then with an elusive lie.

For three days I did not leave the grounds except for an occasional walk to the library. I played cards with the girls on the hot sand of the beach. Colleen taught me to pick out a few tunes on her guitar during the long quiet evenings. I settled those frequent arguments between Ellen and Frieda, and I listened to Joan's wailing with a forced patience. And I knew why I did all this—to recapture the old, monotonous life, to drop back into the waiting that centered around Phil, and to forget as best I could that I would not see Hank McKellar again.

Colleen noticed the change. "You should find something," she said. "Something to do with yourself."

"We're not all as lucky as you."

"No ... no, I guess I am lucky."

And she was. For in a way, Colleen Sims was the best-adjusted of all us girls. She used her time to some purpose by going down to the San Diego naval hospital three days a week. She'd even found a particular young marine who more or less depended on her visits in order to get well again. He was an amputee, convinced he would never learn to walk, depressed, bitter, sure no girl would ever want him. According to Colleen, she'd cheered him up considerably. She'd even taught him a few chords on the guitar.

Yes, Colleen was the most constructive of us all. She came from Oklahoma, where her husband had run a hardware store. Now he was a sergeant in the army, serving in Korea. Colleen had left Oklahoma immediately after her husband had gone overseas. She'd tried for night club jobs along the California coast, failed, and finally landed in Salamanca—depressed, discouraged, feeling as useless as all the rest of us.

But Colleen had found a way out, helping herself and her country as well. And to justify us other girls, I'd like to point out that it's difficult to find some way to help when your country's at war. You give blood every six weeks or so, then comfort yourself with the false reasoning that you've given your husband and you're suffering enough.

During those three days of trying to forget Hank McKellar, however, I began to realize that if I had found something constructive to do in the beginning, then I would not be hiding now—from either Hank McKellar or myself—and I would not be writing evasive lies to Phil. A heavy sense of guilt started eating away at me, heightened each time Colleen went off with the guitar under her arm, each time she returned with her latest enthusiastic news about how her special patient, Paul Sarkis, was getting on.

"He'll be ready for artificial legs before very long, and I feel almost as if it was myself. I don't know ... he's like a kid brother. I never had a kid brother, and ... well ... it's wonderful, that's all. It's wonderful."

I did not quite believe her, and decided to see for myself how really wonderful Colleen's life was, how really well she had solved this problem of waiting it out. So one day I took a bus to San Diego, then a taxi to the hospital. I had not told Colleen I was coming, and had no plan in mind except to see where she went and what she did. It seemed impossible for a girl to find

contentment so easily. And actually, I suppose, I was almost hoping to find that Colleen was merely attempting to fool herself,
that underneath she was as discontent as all the rest of us.

The head nurse at the hospital recognized Colleen's name
immediately. "Colleen Sims," she said, "Oh, yes—in room 4A.
Just follow the guitar music." And she smiled and added, "She's
done that boy a lot of good."

"I know."

"Paul Sarkis. Very young. It's hard to lose both legs when
you're very young." She frowned a little, then waved me down
the linoleum-covered corridor.

I walked slowly, trying to keep my heels from clicking. I
peered through the open doorways at the sick and wounded in
their white iron beds, feeling that awe I always felt in the quiet of
a hospital, smelling that peculiar odor of antiseptic cleanliness.
I rounded a bend and heard music—guitar music—and the soft
voice of a girl singing. And leaning against the wall near an open
doorway was a short, dumpy-looking nurse. She wore no make-
up. Her hair was in strings, her face flat with bushy eyebrows,
her legs thick in cotton stockings. I moved closer and she looked
up quickly with suspicion and resentment. I stopped then, quite
close to her. The music was louder now, and through the doorway I could see the angular body of Colleen. She was sitting on a
white bed, her good legs curled under her. She sang softly, strumming the guitar while the boy in the bed lay quiet with his eyes
half closed, a tiny smile in the corners of his young mouth.

I watched them a moment. I saw a contentment on Colleen's
face that was new, deep, more real than that of any girl I had
seen in Salamanca. And standing there in the doorway, I finally
understood why Colleen came here so often, and why she needed
nothing else in her life of waiting. She'd left Oklahoma with
boots, a guitar, a ten-gallon hat—and too much ambition. She'd

failed in all her attempts to find a cheering audience that would call her back for encore after encore in the larger theatres or the better clubs. She'd landed in "the girl cage" along with the rest of us, and finally, here in this naval hospital, she had gained a small but important triumph that substituted for all that she'd missed. Her audience, her public, her very life had reduced itself to a leg-less marine private by the name of Paul Sarkis.

I turned away, realizing my presence would do more harm than anything else. I walked back down the corridor with the squat nurse's eyes following me. And after I'd turned the bend, her voice sounded harsh behind me. I stopped, turned, watched her waddle toward me down the linoleum. "Yes?"

"You know Mrs. Sims? Colleen Sims?"

"Yes.…"

"Did you know she was a distracting influence around here?"

"Distracting?" I was surprised. "Distracting?"

"It would be better if she stayed away."

"I don't understand. The head nurse—"

"What does the head nurse know about it? It would be better if Mrs. Sims did not come here again, and I'd appreciate it if you'd tell her so."

I felt quick anger then. I said, "Why don't you tell her so yourself?"

"I have. But she won't listen." The plump nurse glanced at me scornfully, brushed back the strings of hair across her forehead, and stomped back down the corridor.

I looked after her, puzzled. Then I shrugged and went out to the daylight once more. I took a cab and stared absently out the window. Passing the naval depot, I noticed the gate through which Hank had driven the jeep that time, and it suddenly occurred to me that somehow there was something wrong in what had happened that night on the beach. Hank was not the type to say he loved a girl without being sure of her answer. He was not the kind to make a pass, accept a rebuff and then just drive her home. There was something wrong, unless ... unless, of course ... he'd really meant it.

I pulled my eyes sharply from the line of docks. Perhaps Hank's ship was still there; and perhaps, by now, it had gone over the horizon with all the others. I did not want to know.

CHAPTER EIGHT

A NOTHER DAY PASSED. Another long week end and the five days to Friday. They were all the same, but I was gaining ground, forgetting Hank a little more in each. Friday started the same, with a visit from a casual friend whose husband had been killed only two months before. She came by to boast that she'd found a marine sergeant who'd tried to sleep with her on the first date. "It's a good sign," she said. "When you're still a virgin, I suppose it's a bad sign. But after you've been married once, it's about the only way a man can let you know how he feels." She stared at me, begging for approval. "You don't understand, Martha. Your husband hasn't been killed yet."

"*Yet?*" I jerked my eyes to the girl's face. "No, I suppose I don't understand." I excused myself, walked up to the library, returned three books and took out four new ones. I bought a windproof lighter for Phil, caught myself wondering whether it would light on a ship's bridge in a heavy gale, then pushed the thought from my mind and walked back through the town. I stopped at the coffee shop, started to enter, but decided against it when I caught sight of all the wives sitting exactly as they had that week or so before, saying exactly what they'd said and thinking exactly what they'd thought. There was no point now in thinking back to a week or so before.

I walked back toward the cottage, and from that moment on, Friday became more than just another day. I sensed it as a cab pulled up beside me when I turned into the gravel drive by the main house. A white-uniformed nurse wearing a cape had stepped out, and now she stood firmly on white-stockinged legs. She paid the driver, then turned to me with her lips compressed, her dark eyes hostile beneath her stringy hair. It was the nurse I had met at the hospital only a week before. She looked me up and down. "Is this the way to Mr. Watkins' guest house?"

I nodded, watching her. I said, "I'm going there myself, if you'd like to come along."

"Thank you." She waddled up beside me, and together we passed between the columns. "I'm looking for Colleen Sims," she said as we walked along.

"Yes ... though she may be out at the moment."

"I'll wait." She said it again with determination. "I'll wait."

We had reached the guest house then, and for a moment we paused on the edge of the cliff, looking down at the group of girls lounging idly on the beach, lying flat with white cotton patches over their eyes. The nurse snorted. "They haven't got much to do, have they?"

"No, I'm afraid not."

"Just come flouncing around the hospital, disrupting everything and everybody without any regard for anyone's feelings."

"You mean," I said carefully, "you mean Colleen, of course."

"Her and that guitar!" The nurse stomped into the guest house, lowered herself to the leather hassock, then stood again and paced back and forth on her short legs.

"Would you care for tea?" I asked.

"No, thank you."

"Coffee then?"

"I came to see Mrs. Sims. You see, I know it is *Mrs.* Sims." She looked up suspiciously, biting on her pale lip. "You've been to the hospital. You know about that amputee, Paul Sarkis. I saw you there myself."

"Yes...."

"And Mrs. Sims told you he was depressed when he first arrived at the hospital, didn't she? He had some idea no girl would ever want him?"

"She implied that."

"Well, now Paul's convinced that a pretty girl *would* want him. One who plays a guitar ... by the name of Colleen Sims."

"I see...." I sat. I lit a cigarette, glanced up to find the nurse watching me with the hostility fading from her black eyes. "You mean, of course, that since Colleen is married, there'd be no ... well ..."

"I mean she lied to Paul. She made him think she wasn't married, and—"

"And I let him think so because the head nurse advised it." The voice was low, almost threatening. Colleen moved into the doorway, leaned back against the frame, and stared at the nurse. "I expected you'd be around sooner or later. What do you want anyway?"

"What do *I* want?" the nurse said; "what do *you* want?"

"Just the satisfaction of making Paul feel that someone's interested in him. After all, he's very young and—"

"Very young. Oh, very young!" And suddenly the nurse laughed. It was high, almost hysterical. "Just young enough to think maybe you'll marry him. But you didn't think of that, did you? Oh, no, you come prancing around, singing your cowboy songs, being the sweet little entertainer, while all the time he's falling in love with you." She paused, drew a handkerchief from her white-starched pocket, and blew her nose. "And he was getting along fine too. Before you came along, he was getting on fine."

There was silence then. The nurse put away her handkerchief. I snubbed my cigarette, hesitated, and lit another.

Colleen moved farther into the room, wetting her lips, hunching her shoulders. She came very close to the nurse's seated body, leaned over, and said, "What have you got to do with this?"

"I—"

"You're in love with him, aren't you? You're in love with him."

"So what if I am?" with her voice cracking.

Colleen laughed. The sound was unpleasant, like the words that followed. "And do you know how he feels about you? You've embarrassed him, made him miserable. You've spied on him and discouraged his seeing me or anyone else for that matter. Is that your idea of being in love with someone? Trample all over him, shut him away from even—"

"And what about me?" The nurse stood. She was short, reaching only to Colleen's shoulder. She drew her lips in tight so they disappeared completely, then spit out the words. "He's going to marry me. That's what about me ! And do you know why? Do you?" shrieking then, until suddenly her stubby fingers ripped at the white cape, flung it open, and her hands touched the stiff cloth over her stomach and she shrieked, "You think I've always been fat like this? You think my stomach is always this big? Well, it isn't, and it wasn't until Paul came along. But now you've gone and ruined everything. Now you've—" And she stumbled for the door, tripping over the cape, pulling it from under her feet so that it ripped, making a sharp tearing sound in the sudden silence. And then in a moment she was gone, waddling along the cliff, trailing the white cape behind her until she disappeared among the trees.

"Well!" Colleen sat, stood up again. "Well." She picked up her guitar, struck a chord, then suddenly flung the instrument to the sofa. "That's that."

"Look, Colleen—"

"Try every club from here to San Francisco, end up in a hospital as an amateur entertainer. Then—"

"It can't be helped."

"You never really understood, did you?" She picked up the guitar, put it down, stood with empty hands like a mother who has lost a child. She laughed nervously, said, "I think I'll have myself a drink," and strode into the kitchen. There was the sound of an opening refrigerator, the sound of a clinking glass and the sound of a girl crying, all coming together beneath the swinging door.

I went to my room, slipped into my bathing suit, and returned to the living room. Colleen was sitting on the hassock, holding a glass in both hands. "That's that," she murmured. "That, Mrs. Colleen Sims, is that."

"Look," I said. And then because there were no words to say, I continued out through the doorway, across the lawn and down the wooden steps to the beach. There the women still sprawled in their brief bathing suits with their eyes fixed absently on the ships passing slowly down to sea over the rim of gray water.

"Well," a girl said, laying down her gin rummy hand. "Well, I guess that's that."

That's that. It went round in my head as I lay back on the sand. *That's that.* And I rolled over on my back and looked up at the sky and the cotton puffs of clouds.

A lot of things were *that* for me as well as Colleen Sims. I felt the warm sand against my skin. I closed my eyes against the sunlight. Hank McKellar was *that* for me. I'd sat here on this same beach on a quiet night, and Hank McKellar had said, "I'm in love with you," and he'd looked at me seriously in the half-darkness. And he'd gone, and that was that.

I rolled over on my stomach again. Why hadn't I felt ashamed? I still did not know for sure. Because after what I'd expected from

Hank, his simple, almost naïve approach had seemed so terribly innocent. But that was not *exactly* it. Not *exactly*. All I knew for sure was that despite the guilt, I still was not ashamed, and that Hank's going had left me relieved and somehow discontent in my careful return to the old life of waiting, as though some new emotion had started deep inside me, to be cut off sharply, leaving me very naked and very much alone.

I heard the slap of cards, the high chatter of women's voices. Then the sun was shaded from my back and a nasal voice said, "Mrs. Gwynn."

"Yes...." I rolled over and squinted up at the grinning yellow face of Koko, Lloyd Watkins' Japanese houseboy.

"Message for Mrs. Gwynn," he squeaked.

"Oh?" And I sat up, hugging my knees.

"Message say Mrs. Gwynn come to Corsair Hotel. Message from Lieutenant Hank McKellar." Then he beamed and turned on his bandy legs. He looked like a white-coated spider climbing the long wooden stairs.

CHAPTER NINE

FOR A MOMENT I did not move. I rocked back and forth in the sand, looking out to sea, wondering what I ought to feel, what I really *wanted* to feel, and thinking rather foolishly that I'd known Friday would be different all along. Then I pulled slowly to my feet, gathered my magazines and suntan lotions, and moved after Koko up the stairs to the guest house. I knew I would see Hank McKellar, but there was still nothing but apathy inside me as I dressed in a yellow cotton with bare shoulders and a halter top, sprayed perfume behind my ears and made my mouth up carefully. I brushed my hair, and it was then, performing that repetitive task, that emotion first came. It was anger—dumb anger in my jerking hand, blind anger that grew inside me as I strode down the gravel drive, through the shaded trees to town.

I had almost adjusted myself to what had happened between myself and Hank McKellar. I'd wondered at it, been frightened, awed, relieved, and disturbed by it. And in the end I had learned to accept it. Now Hank was back, hardly more than a week later, sending me messages from the Corsair, where Frieda met with her Major Mullins. He was asking to see me as though nothing had happened, as though the spark had not already fallen and been abandoned. I let the angry resentment creep over me until it became a part of my body, there in the slightest move I made. It was there in my walk as I strode across the Corsair's lobby, there in my hand as I clenched the house phone between stiff fingers, there in my voice when I said, "What do you want from me now?"

"Hank McKellar's buying drinks for all—"

I slammed down the receiver, stood biting my lip, thinking, "He's got to get out of here! He's got to leave this town and stay out of this town! I won't have him doing this! I won't, I won't!" And I kept saying it under my breath as I stepped into the elevator, stood taut until the door slid open, then walked down the carpeted corridor to his room. I paused before the door, then raised my angry fist and pounded four times.

The door swung in, and there was Hank McKellar, grinning down at me. He'd been drinking, and his unruly hair was down in wisps over his high forehead. One hand clutched the edge of the door, and one shirtsleeve was unbuttoned so the cuffs flopped about his wrist. "A real pleasure," he said.

"It's all yours." I looked down at the glass in his hand. "You're buying drinks for all navy lieutenants named Hank McKellar." And I moved past him in the room, past the table of ice water and glasses and half-empty bottles of bourbon. I braced my hands on the window sill, stared down over the town of Salamanca, where the sailors danced like small boys in sailor suits in the street below. "I came here for one reason," I said out of the window. "To ask you to get out of this town—go back to San Diego and stay there, and stop acting like a college boy."

"Want a drink?"

"The last time I saw you, down there on the beach—that was the end of it. I had a nice feeling about you after you'd gone. Now you'd like me to remember it as something pretty sordid, wouldn't you?" I felt his presence behind me and turned sharply and walked away from him. "I don't know what you want, Hank."

"I'm in love with you."

"I said I don't know what you want."

He did not answer. He poured a drink, waved it toward me, and when I shook my head, he drank it quickly himself. "All right." He banged the glass to the table. "A guy knocks around the world until he's pushing thirty. He gets himself in and out of bars and parlors and bedrooms and whore houses, and he keeps going in and coming out because there's always a chance he might stay, sometime. Finally he decides to be a nice boy, so he sits at a quiet little table in a perfectly decent hotel, and along comes a girl who sits down with him. He likes her. They're *simpatico*. He can't stop thinking about her. The bars and bedrooms are suddenly no fun, and worst of all, they're not even temporarily satisfying."

"There's more to it than that. You're not telling me everything."

"I'm not?"

"No, there's something queer about you."

"Sure, I'm a pansy."

"Hank—"

"All right, I'm a pimp. I smuggle young wives into Mexico." He laughed and poured another drink. Then he looked directly at me and said, "What do you suggest about us?"

"I'm married, Hank."

"I asked you what you suggest."

"I suggest you get out of here and keep going."

"How do you feel about it?"

"I suggest—"

"How do you *feel* about it?" He set the glass down carefully this time and moved toward me slowly. The hair was still across his forehead. The sleeve still flopped at his wrist. He was tall, and seemed to grow taller as I backed away. Suddenly my hands were behind me, bracing me against the wall. My head was tilted far back, my eyes drawn to his—more intense and frightening now than ever. He moved close and placed his own hands flat against the wall, fencing me in. I wet my lips. I said, "Hank—"

"I'm not interested in reasons. Just how you *feel* about it."

I could not have told him exactly how I did feel, even when he pulled me in close with his strong arms and kissed me hard, with his teeth bruising my lips--—even when I was involuntarily responding, darting my tongue against his, trembling all through my body while his hand slid down the neck of my dress.

My hand reached out and pushed the hair from his forehead. "Hank!" I jerked away and started for the door, buttoning my dress.

"Get out of here! Get out, get out!"

My hand trembled on the door knob. I pulled the door wide, strode to the elevator and stood there with my heart pounding while I watched the lighted arrow over the sliding doors. And I did not breathe again until the car stopped in the lobby and the door swung open, letting me free. For a moment I paused, lost, looking for direction. Then I turned and walked through the lobby to the air-conditioned bar. I sat at a corner table, ordered a Tom Collins, and drank it slowly, waiting to be myself again. It was good to feel the cold glass in my hand; it was good to feel the cold air of the bar against my face. I had two drinks, then moved out to the lobby. As I stood buying cigarettes, I felt a gentle tap on my shoulder.

Frieda spoke low, confidentially. "I saw you come down, Martha, and—you know something? *I* haven't been upstairs in this hotel since the day we all went to the Beach Club."

"Well," I said, and then added flatly, "Good for you."

"Don't you think it's shocking the way that little bellhop is always hanging around? I mean, did you notice how there's something so sordid about hotel rooms anyway?" Then she frowned a little and said, "It does make it hard, though. I mean you have to go *some place*, and ... well ... we could share an apartment between us...." And she was still talking on when I turned and walked out into the late afternoon, past a number of vaguely familiar figures on the cool of the Corsair's terrace, past the admiring sailors who lolled aimlessly beneath the striped awning of the drug store, down to the sand that was still warm from the day's early sun. The habitual afternoon bathers were gone, but Joan was still in the water, the white parts of her bathing suit clenched wet and small in each fist. She looked up as I drew near, ducked under water, came up, and ducked again. Then she waded to the sand, shaking her head, dancing on one foot.

"Water in my ear." She laughed awkwardly.

"Yes, it happens sometimes."

A pause while her bare toe dug into the sand. "You saw, didn't you? You've known for a long time."

"Yes...."

"But it makes you forget. I mean, you might go crazy. I mean, swimming like that makes you forget about your husband, and—well—I mean you have to forget." Her pale eyes raised defiantly, then softened as they met mine. She was embarrassed, and frightened. Her lips trembled, and then she mumbled something and walked past me down the beach toward the secluded end of the cove. Her shoulders moved as she dragged along, as though somewhere inside her she was crying.

I stood in the red of the dropping sun. I stared out to sea, down at the imprints of Joan's bare feet in the wet sand, along the beach to the girl's body growing ever smaller. Finally I turned, and my legs pulled me up the wooden stairs. Anger was still inside me. Anger and confusion and a horrible sense of help-lessness. At the top of the stairs my feet stopped in indecision, and my body swung easily from side to side like that of a ballet dancer. Then my indecisive foot moved out of its own accord, and I stumbled forward through the eucalyptus trees toward the big glass house and the sound of cocktail laughter behind the big glass windows—toward the sound of voices and the company of people who could not touch me.

Koko answered my ring. He seemed surprised, since I'd been avoiding Lloyd Watkins for weeks, avoiding his eyes that undressed me and the superior twist of his smile. Koko raised his thin eyebrows. "Mrs. Gwynn," he said, and pulled the door open wide.

Behind Koko in the long, glass-walled living room were the voices of Lloyd and Ellen Joslin. Colleen was there too, quite drunk, strumming her guitar, trying to make a fox-trot of the "Missouri Waltz," then giving up and swinging into the pounding rhythm of "Old Soldiers Never Die."

"But what about their wives?" I walked into the room, aware that my voice was too cheerful, my smile too bright. "What about old wives and young wives and middle-aged wives? Do they ever die, or do we all just fade away?" And yes, I'd have a martini, very dry please. Yes, I'd just been for a walk, that's all. I'd been reading on the beach and decided to go for a walk. Yes, it was a bore, but then what could you do about it? You could have a martini, and you could sit and feel Ellen's jealous eyes staring at you from across the room.

Lloyd put some old Bessie Smith records on the phonograph. Then he danced with Ellen. Or rather Ellen danced with Lloyd, using her hips mostly, her feet barely moving. And then Lloyd danced with me. His fingers dug into my back. He held me in close against his chest and said, "You're twenty-three, is that right?"

"Nearly twenty-four."

"Nearly twenty-four, nearly twenty-four." His thigh touched mine. I moved away and felt Ellen's eyes burning into my face. I wondered what it was that she saw in Lloyd—what kept her constantly this way, glowering, ugly, jealous of everyone, as though she had Lloyd for herself, yet hated herself for that fact that she wanted him at all. And I wondered at my own queer feeling that Lloyd did not really want Ellen, or me, or any girl at all.

Lloyd caught me watching Ellen. He said, "Ellen—you understand about Ellen? I mean—"

"I don't care to understand."

"And you're only twenty-three."

"Yes...."

"Ellen's thirty." Then a pause while the music came to an end, and then his pale eyes stared down into my face, dropped to my mouth and the neck of my dress. "Oh, Lord," he said, "Oh my God!" I pulled away and poured another martini with a shaking hand.

Then Colleen wanted to make an announcement. She staggered to her feet and mumbled that in Tiajuana on Saturday there were very fine horse races, and in Tiajuana on Sunday there were very fine bull fights. She saw no reason why we shouldn't all go down to the fine horse races and the fine bull fights, a matter of only twenty miles to the Mexican border, a matter of only a few more miles across that to the charming little prostitute- and sailor-infested town of Tiajuana. She'd heard of a fine little hotel called the Hosteria del Sol where we could have fine connecting rooms, and where tequila was served in the finest glasses we ever saw.

It was all a very fine idea, except that Ellen decided that she and I should change our clothes and bring along the few odds and ends that girls brought along on such occasions. Colleen wanted nothing but her guitar. So Ellen said we'd be right back, and led me uncertainly toward the door. Koko stopped us with fresh drinks. It seemed a good idea to take one along while packing and changing clothes because if you didn't, you might change your mind about it's being a fine idea. If you changed your mind you'd probably go anyway, but wouldn't enjoy it. So why not enjoy it, since you were going anyway?

All the way to the house Ellen squeezed my arm. "Have a great time," she kept saying. And then in the living room she said, "But if anyone wants to start something, I'll tear her eyes out with my bare fingernails."

I set my martini on the wooden mantel of the field-stone fireplace. I knew I would go to Tiajuana with them. If Hank would not leave, then I would leave, if only for a week end.

Ellen sang as she dressed. Joan came in from the beach.

"I see you're having a cocktail," she said.

"Yes."

"I knew you would."

"You knew I would what, Joan?"

"Oh, I just knew you would." She looked at me again in that odd, pleading way, then passed through the living room down the small corridor to the doorway of her room. A light switched on and with it Joan's voice rose in a scream with the words barely distinguishable in their hysteria. "Get out! Get out!" lifting to a crazy wail that rose and fell and rose again as Frieda and her embarrassed Major Mullins pushed out to the corridor. Frieda was pulling on her dress, muttering, "Do I have to buy a house? Where *are* we supposed to go?" And the major was swearing, buttoning his shirt. He strode down the corridor with Frieda behind him, out through the living room and fast across the lawn. Joan lay face down on the bed. She kicked her feet and screamed into her pillow, "My own bed, my own bed!"

I stood silent a moment, then moved into the room, lifted my suitcase from the closet, and packed it quickly. I looked at Phil's picture on the dresser, at the new wind-proof lighter I'd been saving to give him personally. I picked up the lighter, dropped it into a drawer.

Joan was sitting motionless in a straight-back chair, her eyes fixed on the indentation of two heads on her single pillow. She kept talking all the time I packed, her voice dropping from a scream to a whisper, so that she barely moved her lips. "My own bed, my own bed. Almost the same. Almost the same," talking with fascination and revulsion, talking absently of some time in the long ago, saying, "It was late when we left the dance … at the Congregational Church, and it was late. But he didn't take me right home, because first we had barbeque sandwiches in the car at one of those roadside stands, and then we took a short drive through town, and then Ned turned down the road to the house. But he didn't turn in the drive. He just switched off the lights, and we sat in the car and finally he said, 'Shall we walk around a little?' And I said, 'Why not?' So we closed the car doors and walked around near the house, and then down past the barn. And we laughed and spoke to the horses, and then we walked by the edge of a cotton field, and we picked the white puffs as we moved along.… I said, 'It's fun, isn't it?' And he didn't say anything. He was brooding and he tore the cotton balls into pieces and tossed them about like big snowflakes.… So I said, 'Look,' and then I said, 'Listen—' But I didn't know exactly what I wanted to say.…

"And we walked into the woods beyond the field right to this clapboard cabin. And it was my own cabin really, because Daddy built it there for me to play house in when I was little.… Anyway, I laughed and said, 'This is *my* cabin—sort of specially mine.' And I pushed open the door so the moonlight was right there in the room. And I said, 'This is *my* chair, and *my* table, and *my* bed.' Then he said, 'Just like the three bears,' and he laughed, somewhere down low in his throat.… So then we moved about the room and we touched all the books and the toys left over from when I was little.…

"But something was crazy inside me, and I giggled a lot, and when it seemed time to leave, I just stood there wetting my lips and saying, 'Well—well—' Then he said, 'Well?' And I said, 'Well, shall we go now?' And he said, 'Yes, I guess we'd better go now.' But I just stood there all the same, so when he came toward the doorway, there I was, blocking off the moonlight.... So he stopped and put out a finger and touched the sleeve of my dress. And he said, 'Well—' again, and then 'Joan ... look, Joan....' while the moonlight seemed to push us together. So we kissed and we stumbled to the bed, and his hands unbuttoned my dress and they were trembling when he touched me.... And I guess it was all kind of awkward because it was the first time and even the first night I ever met Ned. And anyway he couldn't find me, and he pulled away from me right afterwards, and then he dressed with his back turned and he said he loved me. He said he was sorry too, because he knew it wasn't supposed to be exactly this way, not *exactly* this way. But he couldn't help it and it was the first time for him too, and he loved me and—well, he was sorry.... I said, 'Please don't be sorry.' That was all I said....

"And then he left and I saw him in the doorway and heard his feet on the path. And toward the end I could have sworn he was running.... Then for a long time I just sat on the bed and listened to my heart and all those little sounds of night ... until finally I got up and patted the bed and said, 'My bed.... It's my bed,' and I walked back along the cotton field and past the barn where the horses were rustling the hay and the barn floor was creaking under their weight...."

Joan paused. Her voice died away to nothing. Then it came back stronger than ever, saying, "My own bed. Sort of specially mine," going on again, while I lifted the suitcase and went out through the door, across the bluff and through the woods in the late afternoon.

Lloyd was standing by the open door of the Jaguar. Colleen was in the back seat, strumming a meaningless tune. Lloyd told Colleen to please shut up. He looked at me as I climbed in and said, "Oh Lord, oh my God!"

"Don't say that, Lloyd! Just don't say that!"

"Should have seen her," Colleen said. "Fat, stringy hair, bushy eyebrows. Crawled right in that nice hospital bed with him. Can't imagine—can't imagine—"

Lloyd started to laugh, but then Ellen approached through the trees, and he turned to her, forcing a smile. "Well, we were waiting for you."

"A little trouble," Ellen said. "Poor Joan. She always did shock easy."

"Trouble?"

"Nothing she won't cry herself out of."

"Nothing you can't drink yourself out of," Colleen said.

Lloyd laughed, got into the car, turned the engine over, and started down the drive. I leaned back in the rear seat. Rounding the bend in the drive, I noticed that the sun had gone almost entirely into the sea. What was left was a blood red. It stabbed like a hot knife against my eyes.

CHAPTER TEN

N ONE OF US got to Tiajuana, and I did not travel beyond the columns at the end of Lloyd's drive. For as we swung off the gravel to the winding macadam road, a small boy on a bicycle wobbled from among the trees and passed directly in front of the car. Lloyd jammed on the brakes, the tires squealed, the car lurched toward the ditch. The boy fell off his bicycle and sprawled on the pavement. He wore a Western Union hat, and it rolled as he fell.

Lloyd swore violently. The boy stood and dusted himself off. He looked frightened and embarrassed. He didn't know whether to stay or ride away fast on the bicycle.

I opened the car door and said, "Are you hurt? Are you all right?"

"Yes, ma'am." His face was freckled. He looked like a very young Mickey Rooney. "I got a telegram," he said, stuttering, glad of some reason for being here at this moment. "Mrs. Frederick Crocker. I got a telegram." He reached in his pocket and drew out the crumpled yellow envelope. "See—Mrs. Frederick Crocker."

"Yes," I said. "Yes, I see." I stepped out of the car and took the telegram from his shaking hand. I looked at Joan's married name through the tiny paper window. Impulsively I cupped the envelope so I could see past her name to a word or two of the message inside.

"It's from the War Department." The boy was whispering.

"Yes, I see it is." Then I simply stood there, unmoving. The martinis of only moments before had suddenly lost their effect. I was more coldly sober than ever before in my life.

Behind me Lloyd said to come on. Colleen had started singing again. "You go along," I told them. I gave the boy a quarter and smiled and watched him wobble away on his bicycle. "Go on," I said again, talking to no one, just saying words. Then I turned and lifted my suitcase from the car. I looked up and said, "Go on without me." Then I closed the door, turned away, and started slowly back up the gravel drive.

Voices called after me. There was Lloyd, saying, "What in the hell, what in the hell?" There was Ellen complaining that she knew I'd back out at the last minute. And Colleen mumbled that if I did not go to Tiajuana, then she wouldn't go either, because four might be company, but three was still a crowd. They were all arguing as I disappeared among the trees. The last I heard was Lloyd's disgusted voice saying, "All right, we'll drive around and collect a bunch of people and have a party right here. That's what we'll do. Have a big party right here—" And the car swung sharp on the road and disappeared toward town.

All this time I had not thought anything. I had listened. I had noticed the red sun against the windows of Lloyd's house. I had pushed my body forward as though it were wound tight with a key and moved on someone else's will. But now, breaking out from the trees to the bluff and the cottage only yards away, there was nothing more to see or hear, nowhere else to go. "All right," I said aloud. "Keep control of yourself. Don't let yourself go." I looked over the bluff at the beach and the sea beyond, then moved slowly to the top of the wooden stairs. I put down the suitcase and paused, bracing myself against the rail, staring down at Joan's figure on the beach below. She was sitting with her arms propped about her knees. She looked very thin, very defiant, and I thought rather foolishly that of course she *would* be here. After that business of Frieda and the major in her own bed, of course there was nowhere else for her to go but back to the beach, and nowhere to look but out across that deadly sea.

"Well, it's over," I said. "The waiting's over." Then I moved painfully down the stairs. The wood creaked, but still Joan did not turn around. And even when I was close, even then she kept her eyes straight out to sea, purposely ignoring me.

I stood on one foot. I brushed a sandfly from the back of my leg, using the yellow envelope like a small fan. Then I straightened and shifted my weight again, and wished I had not been so curt with Joan only a few moments before. "Joan...." I said it again, softly. "Joan...." And I was crying inside me. "Joan...."

There was no answer.

"Joan, I want to talk to you about something."

"I don't want to talk about it."

"Not about Frieda. Not about what happened in our room. This is something else. A telegram, in fact. I mean it's for you, and—"

"Well, if it's for me, why don't you just give it to me and then go away?"

"Well, you see, Joan—"

"Please give me the telegram!" Her voice was sharp, jerking my hand from my side so the telegram was in easy reach. She snatched it from me.

"Joan," I said. "Listen, Joan...." And then as she tore open the envelope, I let my voice die and only stood there in the sand, watching the back of Joan's head, her fingers carefully folding the telegram, carefully putting it back in the envelope. Her arms moved about her knees once more, and she was motionless, staring out to sea, a thin statue planted there in the cooling sand.

I swallowed. I wet my lips, felt the sun on my uncovered head. I said, "It's hot today. It sure is hot."

"Ned is dead." The voice was a low whisper, like something from the sea itself. "Ned is dead," flat, without emotion. "Ned is dead," repeating over and over like a ridiculous chant. Joan put the telegram away in her beach bag. She stood wavering, and I helped her, finding nothing to say, supporting her with one arm while I collected her beach robe and magazines, and turned with her toward the wooden steps. We reached them after a long time, and she placed one hand on the wooden rail, then took the telegram from her bag and read it again, her lips white, her eyes frowning while she studied the printed words that informed her that Frederick Crocker had been killed in action.

"They told me quick," she said finally. "Quick as the old Ned in telling me that Ned is dead—dead as the old Ned." And then it seemed, then suddenly it seemed that she knew, she fully understood that her Ned—the one who had danced with her that time in the basement of the Congregational Church, the one who had taken a shower with her that time in the El Cortez Hotel, the one she had married and the one she was now waiting for—that Ned was dead. She knew it for certain now. That Ned was dead.

She screamed. The sound was lost among the rocks. Then Joan turned sharply as though listening for the echo of her own wail. She saw the wooden steps still there before her, and she laughed a little and said, "It's a long way up. It's an awful long way to go."

I said nothing. There was nothing to say. I kept my arm around her during the agonizing climb up the stairs. The silence was heavy, suffocating. I couldn't stand it. I said, "I'm sorry, Joan. Really I—" But my voice was only a squeak in a tremendous tomb. I picked up the bag I had left on the top stair. I said, "I changed my mind. Not going to Tiajuana." Then, "If I could only tell you—"

"You're sorry," Joan said. "You're so very sorry." And she laughed again with hysteria there now.

"I'll stay with you," I assured her. "Don't worry, I'll stay with you."

"I don't want you to." We were in the living room then. It looked the same, and yet now somehow everything—everything was different. "I don't want you to. I don't want anybody, not anybody." And Joan stumbled on to her room.

I followed and helped her undress, coaxed her into lying down, covered her with a blanket. She was limp, numb with shock. "You're sure you don't want me with you, Joan?"

"I don't want anybody." Her eyes looked straight ahead for a very long time, and then her tight lips moved almost imperceptibly. "Ned really isn't dead at all, is he?" She smiled then. It was a sly smile, the smile of someone who has outwitted death itself. "For a minute I thought he was really dead, but he isn't, is he?"

"Joan—"

"Funny how you get ideas like that. I've had them for weeks. When his letters stopped coming, I thought he was dead for sure, and it takes a long time to realize you're just imagining things. I mean, you've always told me I imagined too much, and of course I have. So it's just silly to go on thinking—"

"Joan—Joan—" But her eyes had moved slowly to mine. They were still smiling secretly, and I knew then that nothing I could say or do, nothing anyone could say or do, could be of any use at all. I touched her arm. Tears had squeezed into my eyes. I brushed them away.

"Why are you crying?" She was an inquiring child.

"I'm not. I'm not crying." I smiled weakly and left her there in the bed. I closed the door very gently behind me.

Frieda was sitting in the living room when I returned. She was slumped on the hassock, her chin in her hands, her elbows braced against her knees. She looked up slowly, but said nothing.

"You heard?" I said. "About Joan?"

"I heard you talking in there. I can guess."

"Well—" And I waved my hands helplessly and moved to the window, where I braced my hands on the sill and stood for a long time staring out to sea.

Behind me Frieda laughed nervously. "I thought you were going to Tiajuana."

"I came back."

"Sure." And a pause and, "Martha—about what happened with the major. I mean—"

"Forget it." I watched a ship blinking messages back to the naval station. Someone was dead, or perhaps the crew was out of ice cream. The same little light sent both kinds of messages. Like telegrams. *Happy birthday* and *Your husband is dead.*

"Really it wasn't *all* my fault. I mean the major insisted and ..." Frieda's voice trembled and died away. But in a moment it began again, looking for words to amuse me. "But since then, up at the Corsair, I met the most attractive man. Not like the major at all."

"Did you?" I said absently. "Did you meet another man?" I knew she did not want to talk about Joan. She was talking to keep things moving. She was trying to forget and trying to justify herself.

"The major was sore and he went up to his room, so I went in the bar for a drink and there this fellow was. And he was plenty drunk, too. Boy, was he drunk!"

"Oh...."

"Of course I only saw him a minute. But he wasn't like the major at all. One of those guys you have to go after. Tough, if you know what I mean." She laughed, almost hysterically.

"I know what you mean."

"He kept singing the damnedest song over and over again, over and over—'Where do we go from here, boys?' That's the only thing he could say. 'Where do we go from here?'" She laughed again. My body stiffened so that I had to support myself on the window sill. "What?" I said. "What?"

"'Where do we go—'"

"Don't say that, Frieda!" My voice was low, threatening. "Don't say that!"

"*I'm* not saying it. This lieutenant was saying it. This Hank McKellar—"

"Hank—McKellar?" I said it again as though trying to memorize the name. "Hank—McKellar."

"Sure. As a matter of fact he mentioned your name a couple of times. Said he'd met you around and asked where you were. I told him I heard you were going off for a couple of days and—" She shrugged and looked at me slowly and said, "I'm seeing him tonight. We've got a date."

"Have you?"

"I think we'll get along together fine."

"I'm sure you will." I laughed myself. And then, raising my eyes to look at Frieda's bright mouth, her red hair, her lovely and overly-generous body, I felt suddenly sick in my stomach. There was a hard knot in my throat. The question came and hung there trembling on my tongue. "Was Frieda going to sleep with Hank McKellar? Was she going up to Hank's room, that same room where he'd kissed me and pushed his hot hand against my body on this same afternoon? Was she going to sleep with Hank McKellar?"

"What in the world is the matter with you, Martha?"

I started. "Nothing. Nothing at all." Then I laughed and said, "Yes, you'll get along fine together. I think maybe you're just his type." And I turned with a blind haze before my eyes. I stumbled back to the bedroom and lay on my bunk with my face pushed deep in the pillow.

Joan was still awake, chuckling crazily to herself. Something had died for both of us, but somehow I could not seem either to laugh or to cry.

CHAPTER ELEVEN

A SMALL TRAGEDY like the death of Corporal Frederick Crocker made little difference to the town of Salamanca. Joan was only one of many wives. It was too bad her husband had been killed. But on the other hand, the husband of every other wife in town was taking the same chances, fighting the same enemy with the same odds always there against him. And in the same way that soldiers could watch each other die and still move onward, their wives could also eat, drink, and be merry—for tomorrow their husbands might very well be blown to pieces.

So a party was held at Lloyd's home on that Friday night. It had begun with cocktails in Lloyd's living room, gained headway on the defeated start toward Tiajuana, and grown increasingly during the early evening. Many guests were expected to arrive. The party would keep going on its own inertia until it died a dragging, painful death in the early hours of the following morning.

I saw the preparations for that party from the living room of our adobe house. After helping Lloyd round up his guests, Colleen and Ellen had returned for dinner. They were both tight and could not seem to grasp the fact that Joan's husband was really dead. All they understood was that a party had been formed. There was a lot to be done in preparation. Colleen practiced up on a few new songs because obviously she would be asked to play the guitar, and obviously she would oblige. And if she could force herself to get drunk enough, she might even sing a few really bawdy numbers. Ellen spent the entire early evening in the bathtub, doing her best to sober up and cut five years from her age. And Frieda carefully selected the most revealing dress in her wardrobe. It was a white thing with a halter top, making her skin look very brown, her hair very red, her lips very ripe in contrast to the glaring white.

"He'll like that," I told her, keeping my hands clenched stiff at my sides. "Hank will like that."

"Aren't you coming over?"

"No. I'm going to stay with Joan."

"I called Hank about the party, and he asked if you'd be there."

"I won't."

"Said he'd like to see you again."

"Very nice of him." I turned away and spoke over my shoulder. "Isn't he calling for you?"

"No, I'm meeting him in the Corsair."

"The Corsair?" thinking of his room and his eyes and his hot hands all over again.

"He won't come over here. Don't ask me why. He just won't."

I did not answer. I wondered if she were going up to his room. Then I said, "To hell with him," and I made coffee and sat at the table watching the girls dress and leave. And when the house was finally empty, I still sat motionless, listening to the music of Lloyd's early jazz records wailing back to me through the trees.

I hated Hank McKellar. The fierceness of that hatred weakened my entire body, brought a tremble to my hand, a crazy blindness to my thoughts. He had hurt me. He had hurt me and I hated him. And yet, in an odd moment, sitting there alone with the night and the music and the half-crazy girl in the room beyond, I sensed what I had never wanted to admit. Actually, in a physical sense, Hank McKellar had done nothing to offend me. He'd asked me to meet him in his room at the Corsair, and I'd gone of my own will. He'd been drunk and made a pass at me but that, in itself, was no more nor less than any other man would have done under the particular circumstances. So how had Hank McKellar hurt me? And the answer was what I really hated. The answer, rather than Hank himself. He'd hurt me because in my own heart, my own mind, and my own desires, Hank McKellar was more than just another man. And for the first time since college days, I was furiously jealous.

Joan called out from her room. I rose slowly, shaking my head. I went into the bathroom and took two Nembutals from a bottle in the medicine chest. I drew a glass of water, entered Joan's darkened room, and leaned over the bed, where she lay like one in a fitful coma.

"These are sleeping pills," I said. "They're strong, but not dangerous, and they'll make you relax."

"I don't want to relax."

"A good rest, Joan. And tomorrow I'll take care of everything. Call your parents and get reservations and—"

"Why should I go home?" Her voice was quiet, dead. "I don't see why I should go home."

"Well, after all, Joan. I mean after this—"

"After what?"

"Well—"

I looked down at the girl in the half-light—at the blank face and the puzzled eyes and the mouth that kept saying, "I don't understand. I mean, what's all the fuss about? I just don't understand."

"Don't worry," I said, and I slipped the Nembutals between her fingers, coaxed them to her lips, and held the water glass while she sipped. "Now you'll sleep," I said.

Joan did not answer. She lay quiet, listening to the music through the trees, to the long sigh of a ship's whistle out to sea. "Martha—"

"Yes?"

"I don't know why, but I'm—lonesome. I mean I feel like I'm all alone and—"

"I'm here." I sat on the bed and felt her hand on my arm. "Just go to sleep. I'll stay right here."

"You promise?"

"Right here, so just go to sleep." The fingers had tightened on my arm. But they relaxed as Joan's voice said, "You've been awfully good to me, Martha."

"Just go to sleep now."

"No, you really have, and you don't know how much I've needed you all this time." She was silent a moment. Then, "I'll go to sleep. I promise I will if you'll rub my back so I can relax."

"Of course." I pulled down the covers and pushed up her pajama top. Her bare back was thin, her skin like a peeled stick. I rubbed it soothingly, saying "Go to sleep, please, go to sleep." But Joan did not answer. She lay motionless, her head cupped in her arm, until after a long while she rolled over and said, "Martha— you know I—I guess I like you better than anyone." The pajamas were unbuttoned, and her little breasts were like a very young girl's. She touched my hand and drew it down gently until the hand cupped her tiny breast. She was breathing heavily then. She groped in the dark, found the button on my dress and unbuttoned it slowly with stealthy fingers.

"Joan...." There was dryness in my throat. My mind was swimming in sympathy and shock and sudden confusion. "Joan...." But her hand had slipped under my dress while her soft voice begged and pleaded. "I guess I love you, Martha. You don't understand. I love you."

All this time I had not moved. But my mind said, "I can't hurt her now. I can't, no matter what, I can't hurt her now...."

Afterwards I swung my feet over the bed, and strode for the door, trembling all through my body, trembling with horror and helpless confusion. In the living room I buttoned up my dress with shaking hands, started for the door, then hesitated and turned back down the hallway. I peered into the room. Joan lay quiet now, breathing evenly, her face toward the wall. "I'll leave her alone. I can't stay here. I'll leave her alone!" And I turned and went back through the living room, through the trees and past the empty swimming pool toward the house and the music and the laughing people.

The music grew louder as I approached. A group of guests stood under the portico. They were drinking, laughing, telling stories. I paused in the darkness, wanting time to think, time to think, time to think. Yet really I did not want to think at all. And I strode hurriedly through the knot of guests and through the open doorway to the living room.

A highball was pushed into my hand. I took it and stood in a far corner, my eyes moving slowly about the room. Lloyd was very drunk. He was talking to a dark-haired, dark-eyed sailor, while Ellen stood beside them, clutching Lloyd's arm, urging him to dance. Colleen sat alone on the sofa, absently strumming her guitar, stopping now and then to beckon Koko over with a fresh drink. And everywhere—on all the chairs, in all the corners, in all the rooms, was laughter and anger, the click of ice, the smell of smoke, the same old brittle voices from the same old bored and brittle people. "Tell you what I think," and "Little air, let's go for a little air," and "Drink, please," and "Sleep with you, please.... Drink, please, sleep with you, please...." so that all conversation meant exactly that. Talk about the weather and it meant exactly that. Discuss politics and it meant exactly that. "Drink please ... sleep with you please...."

"God!" I told myself. "God!" And I knew, saying those words, that something was missing. I knew what that something was—Frieda Doyle and Lieutenant Hank McKellar.

I accepted another drink. The jealousy came back and burned behind my eyes. It moved my legs slowly through the room, into the dining room, the kitchen, past the row of bedrooms from which giggles and laughter seeped out beneath closed doors, out to the rear of the house and the darkened solarium, where two familiar figures stood close and two familiar voices spoke softly in the dark.

"I told you I let one of the men take the jeep." And that was Hank McKellar.

"We can walk, can't we?" Frieda was coaxing, wheedling. "It's not very far to the Corsair and—

"And what do we do when we get there?"

Frieda laughed. "God!" she said.

"Sure." And Hank's voice was quiet now. "But maybe I've got some ideas of my own."

I did not hear the rest. I turned and carefully retraced my steps, back down the corridor and through the living room, out to the drive and through the trees to the swimming pool. I sat on the concrete edge, trying to calm my mixed emotions—the horror of that experience with Joan, the unwanted rage and jealousy I'd felt concerning Hank McKellar, and this strange relief, knowing he was still close, even with Frieda, he was still close. The end was not yet quite in sight.

I was still sitting there when two dark figures appeared through the trees. Both were men, though I could neither see their faces nor hear their words. They stood close in the garden beside the swimming pool. They were talking in low voices, laughing now and then, until gradually the laughter disappeared altogether and there was silence. Someone whispered. Someone gasped. A loud voice said, "What's the idea, you son-of-bitching pansy?" There was the heavy smack of a fish against flesh. Then another smack, softer this time, and the crash of a body tumbling backward and falling heavily into a flower bed.

I sat motionless, scarcely breathing. This scene was not for me. This was none of my business. And when the belligerent figure strode close by me, heading back toward the main house, I crouched even lower at my place by the swimming pool. But a moon had struggled out by then, and in its half light I recognized the dark-eyed sailor who'd been talking to Lloyd only moments before.

I rose slowly. Behind me another voice, a woman's voice said, "What kind of a man are you? My God, what kind of a—"

Lloyd said, "Ellen—" And then Ellen said, "I don't get it! I just don't get it!" She laughed jerkily. "Because I saw what happened, and what are you, anyway? What *are* you, anyway?" Her voice rose in wild hysteria while Lloyd mumbled on and on, trying to explain what was beyond Ellen's understanding, trying frantically to justify an act he had fought a long time to avoid—an act that had finally been committed, and from here in would make all the horrible difference.

But Ellen would not listen. She screamed in anger and hurt pride. A second later her feet sounded in the brush as she stomped back toward the house.

I sat down again. I waited, but nothing happened. Lloyd was close, but I could not hear him. Finally I rose and moved stealthily back through the bushes. And there, in a tiny clearing, I found

Lloyd Watkins. He was half sprawled in a bed of flowers. He was drunk, and he was crying.

I felt embarrassed and turned away. But his voice called after me. "Martha—please, Martha!"

"Yes, Lloyd?" I looked back at him. He'd struggled to his feet and was bracing himself against a tree. His face was streaked with dirt and blood. "Listen, Martha—listen, Martha—" talking on and on, pleading for me to listen, getting it all out of himself with drunken, twisted words. "Goes back a long way, Martha.... Grandfather very wealthy, Martha.... Pennsylvania mines and a piece of the railroad. Very wealthy, and gave me everything. Private schools, tutors, a sailboat when I was fifteen.... Went to Princeton, read everything and traveled everywhere and tried to experience everything. Wanted to be a writer. Published two volumes of poetry with my own money, then tried the theatre. Producing. Had two flops and tried to buy my way into Hollywood, but couldn't do it....

"I was married, too. She's an invalid. Got drunk one night and I drove us off a cliff. Spinal injury, and she never forgave me. Divorced me and went home to her family in San Francisco, Nob Hill. Built that house for her. Did you know that? In 1940 that was. Then the war and I tried to get in the army and couldn't. Emotionally unstable, the army said. So I lived in the house alone and went crazy. Salamanca was overcrowded with wives, so gave them the guest house. Had four girls in it then, and Ellen was one of them. Husband came back in '45 and they went off to his new base in Norfolk. Then this Korean war, and I opened the guest house again and Ellen came back."

He pushed off from the tree and stumbled toward me. "Can't get rid of her, Martha. Don't you understand? Trying to hold over an affair from the last war. But I've changed since then. Don't want her and hate myself because have to want somebody, and.... Don't you see, Martha? You're beautiful and young and you can help me and some woman's got to help me, got to make me want you—got to help me—"

He was close then, reaching toward me. His face was wild in the dim light. His hands fumbled toward me, touching my dress and leaving a streak of dirt along my breast.

I backed away, horrified at his having wanted me all this time merely to prove his own manhood. Yet the horror I felt was a repetition of another horror, experienced only a short hour before. "Joan," I said, still backing off. "Joan...." Then I turned and stumbled off through the brush, past the swimming pool, out from the patch of trees and across the tiny lawn. Lloyd's hysterical sobbing voice went on behind me. But I did not listen. Suddenly now, I thought only of Joan. I looked toward the house and noticed the light was off in the living room. There was no sound at all. Even Lloyd's sobbing voice had gurgled away. "She's asleep," I told myself. "The light bothered her, so she put it out and went to sleep." I said the words again and sensed the falseness of my own reasoning. Behind me Lloyd's voice rose suddenly in wild drunken laughter, seeming to push me forward so that finally I was running.

Joan was not in her bed. She was gone from her room, gone from the house entirely. I rushed frantically about, then stood panting in the living room and told myself to go at the thing calmly, not to make a lot of foolish phone calls, not to get hysterical. I turned on all the lights. Then I searched Joan's room once more, carefully now. I found her yellow pajamas on the back of a chair. Her bathing suit was gone from the rack on the closet door.

I went out into the night, called into the darkness. Then I moved on to the stairs, and descended them slowly, knowing somewhere in the far corner of my mind exactly where I was going and exactly what I would find. I moved wearily, walking apathetically toward the already known, until I stood there at the water's edge with my body relaxed, my hands hanging loose, my eyes looking down at the two small strips of white cloth that lay on the edge of the water.

CHAPTER TWELVE

PERHAPS IT WAS a long time, perhaps a short time. But in that time I stooped and picked up the white pieces of Joan's bathing suit. In that time I must have screamed, for people came and people went, talking and shouting and moving around me on the wet sand. And in that time I walked with Joan. I heard her voice complain that I had let her down, and Ned should know about this because Ned understood about everything. And I watched her as she slipped off her pajamas and pulled on her white bathing suit. I stumbled beside her through the living room, turning off the lights before moving out to the summer night. I heard the door close behind us, and I walked beside her, barefoot, while the grass tickled our feet as we crossed the short stretch of lawn and moved painfully down the wooden stairs. At the bottom we paused, breathing heavily, listening to the jazz music and the ship's whistle before moving on over the sand that was still warm from the day's sun. It felt good on our toes, and good when we scooped it up and let it trickle out between our fingers. We stood at the water's edge, looking out to the blackness, and Joan said that Ned would be pleased to see her—naked the way she always swam, the way they'd been together in the shower, and the way they'd been together in *her very own bed* in the cabin along the cotton field. I watched her strip off the bathing suit and stand like something from the sea, thin and white. And I heard her say, "I'm going to Ned." And "Goodbye, Martha," and "I'm going to Ned."

I nodded and watched her move out deeper into the sea. I waved and saw her plunge in, heard her gasp for breath, and saw her thin arms rise and fall as she swam into the darkness....

Perhaps it was a long time, perhaps a short time. Still the people came and went. Still I clutched the bathing suit between my fingers. Someone said, "Know anything? Know where she's gone?" And I said, "Gone to Korea. Gone to Ned." And some laughed, and some sucked in their breaths, and some spoke of boats and nets and dragging the green sea. A stout policeman appeared. He waddled up and down on his heels in the wet sand, turning his flashlight down and around, looking for signs of one thing or another. A sarcastic voice said, "Looking for clues?" and it was Hank McKellar's voice.

"You never can tell," the policeman grunted. "The wives around this town get into all kinds of jams."

"Accidents will happen."

"Suicide maybe."

"She liked to swim at night."

"You got to investigate—so the girl's gone and Mrs. Gwynn finds her bathing suit, so you got to investigate."

"Now why don't you go home?" Hank McKellar said. "Take your flashlight and go looking for night crawlers, and tomorrow you can get in some good fishing. Why don't you just leave it alone?"

The policeman said something big and angry, and Hank told him to go home and tell his daughter to be careful about swimming at night.

There were other people around too. But they drifted away one by one. Back to the party, most of them, or back to the apartment or hotel room or wherever it was that they'd come from, until there was no one on the beach at all except this one man, this Hank McKellar, who stood a little apart, smoking a cigarette and swearing softly under his breath. He said, "Martha...." in a low voice. He moved close, and I said, "Please get away from me." But he moved even closer, touched my arm, said, "Listen—"

"Listen, listen—" I laughed and said, "I understand Frieda's been cheering you up."

"Not the way you think. And what did you want me to do—put a candle in my window?"

"I wanted you to get away from me."

"I tried and couldn't make it. Men aren't like you women, you know. They don't weep very prettily. They get drunk and grab on the first whore who'll mother them."

"I don't want to hear about it. I just don't want to hear about it." I turned and walked fast along the sand toward the rocks at the far end of the cove. The pieces of bathing suit were still in my hands. The night was quiet now except for the jazz music that still went on, except for the lapping of the water and the wailing ship whistle that came sporadically, mourning the dead. Something was inside me as I walked. Something walked with me, inside me, that I did not understand except that it was a negative thing trying to become positive. And behind me that man, that Hank McKellar, walked also, silently, saying nothing, with only the crunch of his footsteps behind me in the sand. I said, "I let her down. You wouldn't understand, but I let her down, and then I left her alone. I just walked out and left her alone."

"You're great at walking out. I should know. You're a great little walker-outer."

I did not answer. I had reached the rocks then, and I sat hugging my knees, facing the sea, aware of his tall frame behind me in the sand. I controlled my voice and said, "I hate you. I suppose you know that."

"Yes."

"Did you know I've only really hated one other person? In all my life, only one other person? I was only seven then. In New Hampshire. I'd gone into the woods, and I found a deer there in a clearing. It was dying and it kept looking at me. I sat on a log and watched it die. A boy came along and sat beside me, so we watched it die together. There was nothing I could do, you see. But I thought maybe there was something *he* could do. But of course there wasn't and I hated him for it."

"What do you want me to do?"

"Get out of here. Bring Joan back. Anything except this hanging around tearing the insides out of me."

"Why don't you do something yourself?"

"Oh, I have, I have!" And I laughed again and placed the bathing suit on the sand beside me and thought that I'd bought a windproof lighter and gone to the Beach Club and read a book and had a drink, and there was really nothing else I could have done, except just that—and that was nothing. "I think I'll just hate you," I said. "If you can't get rid of a person, then you have to hate him, don't you?"

"Do you?"

"Yes!" I scooped up a handful of sand, held it clenched tightly in my fist, then flung it away.

"Look," Hank said. His hands touched my shoulders from behind and his voice said, "Cry, Martha. For God's sake why don't you cry, like anybody else?"

"I don't want to cry."

The hand moved down to my throat, and I sat up and turned sharply and swung my fist against his face. "All right, all right!" I jerked to my feet and glared down at him. I wanted to hurt him. I wanted to hurt myself. I wanted to tear something to pieces. My wild, angry fingers touched my dress, ripped the buttons, tore the dress from my shoulders and flung it to the sand.

"Is this what you want?" I said. "After this will you leave me alone?" And then, seeing the pained calm in his face and the tight line of his lips, I bent forward quickly, picked up the pieces of Joan's bathing suit, and held them in front of me. I sat down, half-lay back, looking up at the sky, feeling the cold of the bathing suit and the cold touch of Joan's fingers and the creeping horror that had made me run, leaving the girl alone, making me responsible because of this running—because I was always running. "I'm not running," I said.

"Martha—"

"I'm not running," spoken tight in my throat. He was beside me then, close but not touching me. I turned to him, clutched at his arms. "I'm not running," while a spring snapped inside me and my hands slid along his skin. I felt the perspiration of the warm night on my lips and throat. Suddenly our bodies were straining against each other and my frantic fingers were digging at his back while my voice that was someone else's voice kept pleading, "Kiss me. Never stop kissing me."

CHAPTER THIRTEEN

I FIRST SAW the ranch from the highway that wound along the mountain's edge. It lay small and white with green fields on all sides and big trees hanging their branches over the low roof.

Lloyd eased his foot on the accelerator. "About three hundred acres," he said. "Four horses. You'll have to rotate. Try to get in two a day."

I nodded, my eyes looking into the valley until we'd rounded a bend and the ranch was lost from view. "You're sure it's all right, Lloyd?"

"I told you I hardly ever use the place. Always think I'll move out and be a rancher. Get a lot of horses and all. But then I never do. So exercise the horses and you're doing me a favor."

"Well, if you won't be using it—"

"I told you not to worry." Lloyd swung the green Jaguar onto a dirt road. The car tipped steeply as we rolled into the valley. Neither of us spoke. Lloyd spun the wheel hard to avoid ruts, and I looked out at the brush along the way and told myself that it had worked out very well, and would work out even better in the next few weeks.

Lloyd had suggested the ranch himself. He'd come over to the cottage on this same morning to discuss the business of sending Joan's effects to her family. His eyes had been red-veined, his voice hoarse. Yet he had not even mentioned the night before, and I'd realized then that he did not remember me as a part of last night at all. He'd been drunk. He knew that he'd made the final step toward self-destruction. But he recalled neither me nor the words he'd said. So seeing me then in the morning of a new day, he'd been perfectly at ease. He'd even been surprisingly considerate. And this sudden change in the way he felt toward me was something that even seemed to surprise himself. I'd seen him watching me curiously, probably wondering why he no longer wanted me. And with the desire gone out of him, he'd been suddenly gentle, with no ulterior motives in anything he said. I'd felt more at ease with him then than ever before. He'd said, "You'd better get away for a while. Look like you'll snap any minute." And I'd agreed and he'd suggested the ranch, and even volunteered to drive me down. He'd been nearly enthusiastic, telling me of the old couple that lived near the ranch. They kept the key and took care of the horses. So I'd have nothing to do but get my own meals, keep the house cleaned up, exercise the horses, and think about last night. I had plenty of time to think.

We were passing into the drive then and the house was there before us, small, really, its roof of tile, walls of brick, covered with adobe, with Spanish iron grilles at the windows and an old oak door in front, lugged there from a small Spanish church that Lloyd had found destroyed in Yucatan. The sun was on the endless fields, and only a dog moved lazily on the dusty road.

"Nothing special," Lloyd said, "but I used to be a nut on horses, and it's a good fifty miles from Salamanca, so it ought to work out O.K."

"It's perfect," I said. "It's beautiful." I stepped out and stood looking out over the fields and rising hills while Lloyd drove down the dirt road and returned with the key.

"The old guy," Lloyd said, "his name's Mooney, Walt Mooney, and his wife's Rebecca. Nice people. She'll be down to see how you're making out, and Walt's out in the barn now." He unlocked the front door and carried my bags into the living room. He set them down, picked them up again, and lugged them to the huge bedroom. It was furnished in heavy mahogany, black and intricately carved. There was a mock fireplace and a canopy over the large bed. I unpacked my clothes, slipped into dungarees and a cotton blouse, then went back to the living room, where Lloyd sat sprawled on a bamboo sofa. He was drinking brandy. "Very good stuff," he said. "This Lloyd Watkins fellow is becoming an expert on good brandy."

"Lloyd—you're sure nobody knows where we've gone?"

"Positive."

"I packed and left while the girls were out. I left a note saying I was going off for a while. You can explain some way, but—if anyone knows where I am, then there's no sense in my being here."

Lloyd twirled the ice in his glass. "Don't worry," he said.

"You've been sweet, Lloyd, not even asking questions."

"If I'd known you from the beginning …" he paused and looked away somewhere, "then I wouldn't be gulping this drink and I wouldn't have this black eye." He turned and stared at me solemnly through the swollen eye. "Know how I got it?"

"No," I lied. And then to strengthen my own lie, "Maybe you'd better get back before Ellen starts wondering where you've gone."

"Ellen!" He laughed and stood up. "No more worries about Ellen. In fact she gave me this black eye. I was running away from her and bumped into a sailor's fist. If I hadn't been running, you see, if I'd looked where I was going—"

"I see."

"Do you?"

"Yes, I see."

"If I'd known you from the beginning—"

"You won't tell anyone I'm here?"

"The Watkins word on it. I'm a clam."

"You've changed," I said. "It's as if you've stopped fighting. And all in one night too. As if you fought and lost and suddenly you're a nice guy."

He laughed and I walked to the door with him and touched his sleeve before he climbed into the Jaguar. "Quit drinking," I said. "And maybe you'll see where you're going." I watched him wave and watched the green car creep up the steep hill and turn off and disappear into the mountains.

Mrs. Mooney came over in the late afternoon. She wore an old gingham dress and a beautiful smile. She brought an armful of groceries. She shouted out to the barn for her husband, and Walter teetered in, doffing his hat, wiping the sweat from his forehead. They were fine people, maybe one hundred years old, maybe five hundred years old. Walter seemed older than the land itself, and Mrs. Mooney looked back four generations when her dim eyes turned to mine.

"Your husband's in the war," she squeaked.

"Yes, Korea."

"Nice if he came back and stayed here too. Nice place for a honeymoon." She cackled and left. Walter teetered beside her down the dusty road.

The four horses were all palominos. They lacked exercise and had to be handled with great care. But Walter knew them as restless children. He coaxed me into the saddle and coached me into letting them out easily before giving them their heads to get the sweat up on their flanks and the devils out of their hearts.

I rode fairly well, sitting straight, letting my hair loose in the sun and wind. And I rode far with a fury that made me remember Joan's swimming and made me wonder if perhaps riding horseback were much the same. I found a clear stream that formed a pool at a sharp bend in the rocks. And I swam there, letting the horse rest, letting the cold water wash any creeping thoughts from my mind.

But the thoughts came back. Always they came back. At night, when the house was silent and only the tiny sounds of dark squeaked endlessly outside the iron grille. At the tiny knee-hole desk, where I wrote long and passionate letters to a husband in Korea who seemed almost a shadow now, as hard to know and as hard to love as the shadow of my slow-moving hand on the starched white stationery. The creeping thoughts were everywhere—on the terrace while I read, and in the saddle while I rode, leaning slightly over the horse's neck, talking to him patiently and feeling that I was riding toward something in my life that was always over the very next hill.

The thoughts were unbearable. I'd been unfaithful. Purposely. I hadn't been drunk. I hadn't been seduced. I'd been very angry and violent, and I'd been unfaithful. There was nothing I could do about it. It was something I had to live with until it softened with time. I would write Phil every day and think about him carefully, and tell him everything when the time finally came. I would ride the horses and read the books and swim in the rock-bound pool and wait for Hank McKellar to sail off in his gray destroyer. I would learn painfully. I would learn to live without Hank McKellar. I would learn even more painfully to live agreeably with myself.

There were three days in all. It was a losing fight because physical aloneness could not obliterate guilt, nor squelch desire. It was a losing fight, and I knew it. Secretly I wondered what they were doing back in the guest house—what they were all doing, and what Hank McKellar felt about my disappearance—and what Hank McKellar was going to do about it.

I found out what Hank McKellar was going to do. That was on the fifth day, after my fourth letter to Phil and my fourth guilt-filled night. Old Walter brought me the news as I sat writing at the knee-hole desk. I was engrossed in the lies I wrote, and did not look up when Walter's voice sounded behind me. "Comin' down the road," he twanged. "Seen him get out of a car. Got a bag too."

I laid down the pen, blotted this fifth letter carefully, and turned in my chair before the desk. "Who are you talking about, Walter?"

"Figure it's your husband, I do. Uniform fellow. Walkin' along the road, he is."

"Thank you, Walter." I turned slowly and looked at the old man. He was standing in the hall doorway, scratching his nose, looking for a place to spit.

"Seen him from the minute he got out of the car." He was proud of his old eyes. It was a good half mile, and he wanted it clear that he'd seen it all.

"Thank you, Walter." I smiled, waited. He started to say more, then turned and trudged wearily out through the kitchen. I looked after him thinking that Walter must be close to ninety, thinking that I'd managed four days alone. Subconsciously I'd hoped Hank would try to find me. I wondered now if I were glad he'd succeeded. I did not know. I went back to the letter before me on the desk. It was finished except for the closing. I'd told Phil about the ranch and how wonderful it was for me. I'd told him how much I really enjoyed being alone and thinking of him and thinking of us together. There was nothing more to say. I placed the pen point gently on the paper and wrote, "I love you," then signed my name. I blotted it, folded the paper carefully, slipped it carefully into an envelope and laid it before me on the desk. I had done the best that I knew how. The odds had been against me and I had lost and there was no point in anything now except telling myself that I had lost—and that really, in the heart of me, really I had won.

I stood and moved to the window, braced myself on the sill, and looked out through the twisted iron bars. Hank was walking slowly, carrying the bag with ease. The braid of his hat flashed gold in the afternoon sun. He looked very tall against the fence along the road. Once he stopped to pat the Mooney's mongrel dog. Then he moved on again with the assurance of a man who is walking toward an uncontrollable end that he hates, and will therefore play for all its worth.

I turned from the window, opened the door, and waited with the sun on my face and my body slumped wearily against the frame. Our eyes met while Hank was still yards away, and still they clung as he moved in to me, set down the bag and wiped his face with a soiled handkerchief. "A long walk," he said.

"Yes."

"I should have told the cab driver to come all the way."

"It would have been easier."

He poked a cigarette in the corner of his mouth, lit it, and crushed the match between his fingers. "I took a thirty-day leave."

"Did you?"

"Yeah." He picked up the shabby bag and walked past me into the house. He looked at the living room, nodded approval, then carried the bag to the bedroom, where he unpacked it meticulously. He opened the dresser drawers, peered inside, and closed the drawers again.

I watched him from the doorway. His face was a mask. He took off his jacket and there was sweat on the back of his shirt.

"I think I'll change," he said.

"All right."

"Need some drawer space."

"The bottom two. I need the others."

He did not answer. He placed his clothes very slowly, very carefully in the drawers. Then he took off his shirt and slipped into a clean one. His upper body was brown and hard. He turned slowly and saw me looking at him. He buttoned the shirt and said, "I think you've cried it all out of you."

"Yes, I have."

"I was hoping you would. I've done a little drinking myself."

"About the other night, Hank." I shifted my feet, took a deep breath. "Down on the beach. I'm sorry about that."

"Forget it."

"I wasn't thinking of you at all."

"Forget it."

"Well...." I left the sentence unfinished. I turned from the doorway and walked back through the house with Hank walking behind me. As we stepped out to the afternoon he took my hand, squeezed it hard, and held it firmly as we walked together toward the barn.

"Horses?" he said.

"Yes, didn't Lloyd tell you?"

"Don't blame him, baby. He was drunk. I needled him. He's been drunk for four days."

"I suppose I knew he'd tell you, all along."

"You might have gone to New Hampshire, to your family."

"Then you never would have followed." It was a simple statement, said simply, meaning nothing but what was in the words themselves.

Hank squeezed my hand again, dropping it only after we'd reached the barn and were patting the horses' noses, feeding them dried ears of corn and talking to them in the reassuring language that a horse can understand. Walter stood behind us. He said, "Glad you come, Mr. Gwynn. Sure am glad you come."

"Thank you." Hank glanced at my face, but I was still speaking to the horses as though I had not heard.

"You got back kind of sudden."

"Very sudden," Hank said.

"Well, it's nice to have you." Walter teetered away, picked up a hay fork, and carefully cleaned the floor by the stalls where the hay had dropped from the horses' mouths.

Hank and I went back to the house. We did not speak. We went into the living room, where Hank made drinks and said, "Why don't you take off the dungarees? Put on something pretty and feminine."

"You talk like a husband."

"Do I?"

"Yes, you do." I left the room, changed into a simple white cotton, brushed out my hair, and laid the brush on the dresser beside a brown military brush with the initials *HM* engraved in gold on the dark leather. Phil's windproof lighter lay there beside it. I picked up the lighter, turned, and looked slowly about the room. My heart was calm now. I felt no anxiety, no guilt, no shame—only that there was time now. It had worked out this particular way. I had to have Hank McKellar, and there was plenty of time. I closed my fist around the lighter and went back to the living room.

Hank was sitting in a chair with his long legs stretched halfway across the room. He was drinking a highball and looked as though he'd been living here for years. He turned his head with the same casual ease. His eyes appraised me. He said, "That's the idea. Your husband likes you beautiful."

"I got my husband a present." My fingers relaxed. I held out the lighter, looked at it curiously for a moment, then dropped it into his brown hand. "I bought it especially for my husband. I—I've just been waiting for him to come."

Hank said nothing. He opened the lighter, turned the wheel, polished the stainless steel with his palm, then slipped it into his pocket. I watched it disappear in the brown khaki, and I knew the last thread had finally snapped. I knew quite clearly that I had broken it myself. "My husband," I said. "My husband...."

CHAPTER FOURTEEN

T HERE WAS GAIETY, almost real gaiety, in those long rides
on the dusty roads. We laughed a good deal because Hank
was new to a horse, and it was funny, really, seeing him bent too
far over the horse's neck, with his naval hat on the back of his
head, his khaki pants flopping as he rode. "Sailor on horseback,"
I called him, and raced on ahead, watching him come toward
me, knowing that this was the way it had to be, and that somehow, with God's grace, there would be a good ending sometime,
somewhere.

It was gay and it was quiet, too. For after we'd swum and
splashed and ducked each other in the cold pool at the stream's
bend, then suddenly it was always quiet as we lay in the sun, drying
slowly, chewing a blade of grass, watching a hawk in the sky above.

"I was brought up in Nova Scotia," Hank told me.

He talked slowly, running his fingers along the pulsing
column of my throat. "My father was a fisherman, and always
wanted me to stay there and keep the boat going. I got in the U. S.
Merchant Marine after high school. I liked it right away. The sea's
a terrific place for that—for restless people who don't want to go
anywhere but the ends of the earth."

"So you joined the U. S. Navy during the last war."

"I told you, didn't I?" He sat up and pulled the blade of grass
from his mouth. He crushed it in his hand and tossed it in the
pool of water. His body was brown and hard. His mouth was
hard, too.

"Hank!"

"I told you!"

"You're hard, Hank. You're tough."

He laughed.

"And there's always something you don't say. As if you'd done something—"

"I've never done what I didn't believe. Know any other way to do anything? *Anything?*" He had stood and was glaring down at me. "Do you?"

"No."

"Is this wrong, for instance? Us?"

"I don't know. I—"

"If you don't believe in it, then you shouldn't be here. If you do, then—"

"Then it makes it all right?"

"It makes it the only thing you *can* do—unless you don't believe in it."

"All right," I said. I did not want to talk about it. I'd carefully avoided the moral issues. It was a question of what I wanted and whom I hurt. There was no right or wrong, and I did not want to suspect there ever could be. "All right," I said. "All right."

Hank sat down again. But he did not look at me. He smoked and dropped his voice. "If I weren't tough, I wouldn't be here."

"What does that mean?"

"Neither would a lot of other people."

"Other people?"

"We'd all be dead."

"Look," I said. "Listen, Hank—"

But he refused to say any more. He laughed suddenly, snapped away his cigarette and changed the subject. "After this war we could go to Florida, down on the keys. I've got a little money saved. We could buy a boat. Nothing big. A forty-foot power boat maybe, and take out fishing parties. My father would die happy. It's a good life. You'd like it."

"Yes, I would." And I kept my eyes open, looking into his when he kissed me hard on my still damp lips. He ran his hand lightly and then roughly over my brown body.

It was quiet in the evenings, as we sat in the half-darkened living room, saying little because there was nothing that had to be said. Not even about Phil, because we never spoke of Phil at all. We wanted each other. We accepted that desire, prized it, treated it gently with great respect and even awe. Touching hands was an important event, sometimes planned, sometimes spontaneous. Words were important, delicate things, said carefully in all their forced gaiety. And time was of great importance. There was a lot to say and a lot to do before that crystal time shattered to bits because the wrong word was spoken, because desire had become ever so slightly diminished.

Yet there was something artificial, something *too* fragile about that crystal time. At first I did not realize this. Then, as the days passed, I noticed that we always had a drink or two while we sat and talked during those quiet evenings. Somehow we talked better after a few drinks. We found more truth in our own words. We found more belief in our being together.

Hank said there was no harm in a few drinks. He'd been drinking pretty hard all his life. I was just looking for meanings behind everything. "So we have more fun when we drink," he said. "So why not? Why not?"

"Just once," I insisted. "Let's spend one night without a drink. Just *one*."

He was amused. He agreed. But that night was longer than the others. We found our conversation forced, without conviction. Hank was restless. We argued, and neither of us could get to sleep. We smoked cigarettes and lay apart on the wide bed.

I never mentioned drinking again. I thought perhaps, without knowing it, I'd purposely spoiled that evening in order to prove that it was wrong to drink so much. So from then on we drank a little each noon and a lot each night, getting mellow and keeping the affair going in the easiest possible way.

Yet Hank would not allow me a second of spoken doubt about the fragility of our relationship. "We'll make it," he always said. "We know where we go from here, and we'll make it, and there's nothing to worry about. A fishing boat off Key West or whatever else it is, we'll make it all right. Plenty of sun and plenty of drinking good whisky and making good love. Plenty of everything, and we'll make it, baby, we'll make it!"

He said that in the hot still nights as we lay outside the blankets, sharing a cigarette before turning fiercely toward each other and touching with great restraint. Then we smoked again, letting our fast breathing become slower, touching only fingertips as we passed the cigarette between us.

"We'll make it," Hank said. And he said it at breakfast when we drank gallons of coffee and argued over the day's news and did the crossword puzzles and read the funnies aloud.

"We'll make it," he said—on the horses' backs, climbing the rocks, lying naked in the sun or floating motionless in the icy water, drinking cocktails or highballs, or just suddenly from nowhere, as though it were a poem he had memorized and recited endlessly like a child. "We'll make it, we'll make it."

Even the letters—even Phil's letters could not destroy our passion. I read them alone by the mailbox. They were all the same, those letters, typewritten neatly, hopeful, promising. But I did not permit myself to read beyond the words. I answered them faithfully, avoiding the words I could not bear to write, commenting mostly on what Phil had written, showing interest only in what *he* had done.

Once—only once—Hank said it aloud. "Why don't you tell him now? Write him the truth and get it over with." He was standing behind me while I wrote, and after he'd spoken I laid down the pen and turned deliberately to face him. "Hank—"

"For your own sake."

"You want me, Hank?"

"Are you kidding?"

"Then try to understand. Just try, because if you can't then it's no good. Nothing is any good."

"I understand just one thing."

"Listen, Hank. I'm married. You understand that? It isn't that I'm legally attached to someone. That isn't the point. The point is I met someone I sincerely loved. A nice person, Hank. I married him and I loved him, and we lived together, shared things together." I saw the muscles tighten in his face, and I said, "He went off, Hank, and I suffered terribly. I was faithful and I loved him, and—and then you came along."

"So that's all."

"No, that isn't all. I'm with you, Hank, because I can't help myself. Because some force got inside me, and I can't do anything about it. God knows, I tried. I ran, I fought you, I tried to hate you. I fought myself and I hated myself, and I lost. I lost a fight *not* to think about you. But the fact that I'm right here with you now doesn't mean I've simply ceased to care for my husband. It just doesn't work that way. Maybe in the movies, maybe if Phil were a villain or something. But he isn't. He's a wonderful sweet guy who loves me. And a person that *I* love too. And the only difference is that that love has become overshadowed by the way I feel about you."

"So?"

"So I'm going to treat Phil the way I'd want him to treat me if this thing were the other way around. I'm going to tell him myself, to his face. I'm going to let him divorce me for infidelity."

I stopped, turned slowly back to the letter, and tried to get on with it. But my hand trembled and a blot of ink dropped on the paper. I stared down at the tiny black drop. It did not soak into the glossy paper, but lay there, wet and round like a drop of mercury from a broken thermometer, like a small black crystal ball. Behind me Hank spoke, but in that second my eyes remained fixed on the drop of ink, and my mind tried frantically to understand what this was *really* all about. I'd never told Hank I loved him. Only that I wanted him. There was a great difference. And if love was supposed to be so strong, why was this wanting even stronger? Suppose I'd met Hank in Westchester at a neighbor's party? Nothing would have happened. I was sure of that. So actually it was Phil's absence that accounted for this wild desire.

And what about Phil? I'd told Hank I was in love with my husband, and I was. It was just that time had passed. Phil was an image in my mind—something remembered as a part of laughter, part of crying, part of living. So I loved that image. But the *man* was not here. I could not see him; I could not touch him.

Hank was here. He was real. He was alive. I liked to look at him. I liked to touch him. If that was love, then I was in love with Hank McKellar. Not that I *liked* Hank McKellar. He was evasive, quick-tempered, possessive, and hard beyond any man I had ever known. He'd formed his own values and lived in his own world, created only for people as strong as himself, with no room for the weakness that derives from sentimentality—no room for that weakness that is often a good quality really, because it makes some people a little more kind, a little more sensitive than they might otherwise be.

"Martha!" Hank's voice was sharp, close to my ear.

The blot of ink was completely dry. I slammed my fist against the desk.

"Just don't think about it," Hank said behind me. "Just let me love you and just don't think about it...."

"Just don't think about it ... just don't think about it ... just don't think about it.... Lie there quietly at night, motionless on the crisp sheets, with a moon making a jagged pattern on the side of Hank's sleeping face, with a night bird outside the window and the Mooneys' dog howling endlessly down the road. And just don't think about it...."

The house had been brick and frame, five rooms, a ranchette with a Bendix washer and small fireplace. There were others like it, or nearly like it, all along the treeless street. And there were other men like Phil who trudged to the Westchester station in their gabardine top coats and carefully-polished shoes. There were other wives like myself who waved goodbye from the tiny porch and cleared the breakfast dishes and drank endless cups of coffee during the long day. "Men must work," Phil said, "and women must weep."

"Women must wait." And it was all a waiting because it was all Phil, from waking in the morning, hearing the hum of his electric razor, searching his drawer for a missing mate to an odd sock, getting his breakfast, sitting across from him in the robe that had been beautiful on my honeymoon and was worn now, and not so highly prized. It was all Phil because there was nothing else to want in those days. Only the square boyish smile, and the sight of his rough chiseled face on the pillow, and the way his black hair curled up after a shower, and the way he picked me up in his arms every night when he came home on the six thirty-two and carried me twice around the living room, singing, "Yes, sir, she's my baby."

It was all Phil. We sat at the table after dinner. We drank coffee and Phil said, "So I took this client out for lunch. Razor blades. We're doing some television spots, and I had to butter him up with three martinis before he'd even talk."

"My brilliant advertising executive!"

"Your assistant account rep, who will not get ulcers, who will not get ulcers."

We did the dishes together. I washed; he dried. He was always ahead of me because of his fast, stubby hands. And waiting while I scrubbed at a pot, he stood behind me, playing with the towel. He laid it across my shoulder and slipped his hands about my waist, and didn't mind when I lifted a soapy hand and patted his face, or turned suddenly and put both arms around him and held him close so the soapy water soaked through his shirt and I said, "A clean shirt tomorrow. And it was clean today."

"Twenty cents for a kiss," he said, "and nice men don't wear shirts more than once."

It was not all Phil at those moments. It was both of us, the two of us. The two of us in the living room, watching a television show, the two of us talking of a bigger house on a tree-lined street, and the two of us talking of children, wondering, sometimes even frightened.

"I don't get it, I don't get it. The doctor says we're both big breeders. Why don't we breed? Why not a little breeding?"

"We'll try again," smiling at him until he yawned and it was infectious so that suddenly I was tired too. We stood together. Phil put out the lights. He was first in the bathroom. I always put on lipstick because he liked to see me that way when we awoke in the morning. I returned from the bathroom and found him sprawled on the bed, looking up at the ceiling and smoking. He lowered his eyes and looked at me, and whistled sometimes because I had a body that showed up nicely under a nylon gown.

We never went to sleep immediately. We talked again, of the bigger house, the prospective children, how wonderful life was, how much we loved each other. Then, with the lights finally out, we lay apart, not touching, until his finger played along my arm and my own finger played on his. It tickled. We both shivered and laughed a little until the fingers were hands, moving over shoulders and throats, and the end of a day was there, ending as it should when you were young and very much in love.

Then morning. The sun through the window. Phil's black head on the pillow. His eyes opening slowly, smiling at me. "Good morning, baby."

"I love you, baby."

"You've chewed off the lipstick."

"I love you, baby."

And we lay comfortably, enjoying the early morning, the fact that we were alive and together....

"Just don't think about it, just don't think about it!" I awoke, startled, blinking my eyes. Hank was propped on an elbow, frowning with that hard line along his mouth. It was early morning and the sun was warm through the iron grille.

"Good morning, baby, and you've chewed off your lipstick."

"Hank, Hank, Hank, Hank!" I clung to him and cried a little in the morning.

CHAPTER FIFTEEN

THE HEAT was with us all the way back toward the ranch. The sun burned our eyes and the weariness ached in our bones. Sweat dripped off the horses' flanks, and foam bubbled in the corners of their twitching mouths.

"A shower," Hank said. "God, for a shower!"

Walter took the horses at the entrance to the barn. He held them gently while they drank long from the water trough.

"That's for me," Hank said. "A drink." And he walked on toward the ranch, the naval hat tipped on the back of his head, his shirt dripping with perspiration. I watched him striding along and thought that we'd been here nearly a month now. Hank's leave was almost up. So far I'd avoided thinking of what I would do when he returned to his ship, where I would go when he put out to sea.

Hank went straight to the bedroom, and a moment later the shower was turned on and his voice rose above it as he sang: "My truly, truly fair ... truly, truly fair ... how I love my truly fair!" It sounded ridiculous. Hank would never call any girl his "truly fair." I was not even sure he could ever really love—me or anyone else.

I listened a moment, then moved out to the sun once more, to the twisted letter box that hung by one rusty nail to a post at the side of the road. There was one letter—from Phil—and I opened it as always, standing there in the sun with one elbow leaning on the metal box while I slit the envelope with a fingernail and read the letter slowly from beginning to end. Then I put it back in the envelope, as always, and moved back to the house, as always, following the routine that kept the letter from Hank's eyes and kept Phil's name from coming up between us. The routine was to put the letter in a desk drawer while Hank was still in the shower. I'd done it that way twice a week for nearly a month now, and there was no reason it should not be done that way today. But today the letter stuck in my hand; today Phil was in the hot room beside me, and there was something wrong, something incongruous in Hank's singing voice. I was relieved when the shower was turned off, when the singing stopped. I started to open the envelope once more, then changed my mind. I knew what it said already. I knew exactly what it said, and there was nothing that had not been anticipated. But anticipation was different from fact—and it brought different feelings.

Hank's voice was behind me, "Want the shower? Wonderful! Great!" He moved closer, wearing a huge pink towel around his waist. He kissed the back of my neck. A drop of water fell from his hair and stabbed my flesh like a knife, so I started and jerked sharply away. "Cold," he said. "Great...." But his voice died. He waited. He said, "Something wrong?"

"No...."

"The letter?"

"Nothing."

"It's something. I can tell."

"Nothing we haven't suspected all along." I turned and gave him the letter. "Read it. Nothing personal. Read it."

Then I moved away to the window, where I stood looking out at the mailbox and beyond that to the dusty road that led up steeply to the highway. Behind me Hank was silent. I heard the crackle of folding paper, the slap of an envelope dropping flat on a desk. I heard Hank's voice.

"So what? So he expects to come back fairly soon. So we stay here a week or so more. Then you go back to the guest house and I'll go back to the ship. Then—"

"Then?"

"Then he comes back and you get it over with."

"Just like that—I get it over with."

"Now look, baby—" And anger crept into his voice. "So far we've had all the breaks. This ranch. A thirty-day leave. We've been married. No difference really. Married. And I'll be leaving sometime myself."

"I know...."

"I'll be back."

"Yes...."

"So Phil comes to the guest house and you get it over with. If he can't come there, then you go to Frisco or wherever he comes in, and get it over with. But you *see* him, you *tell* him, and you *get it over with!*"

"I know, Hank. You've said it, Hank." And I was silent a moment, thinking that of course he couldn't possibly realize that we'd been living in a passionate dream, and now reality was stepping in to fight it. And somehow you could not easily fight reality with a dream. It was one thing to lie in the arms of a man you wanted more than anything on earth, while you told each other that this wild feeling was big and could conquer any hesitancy you might feel. But it was quite another thing to face this husband you had loved, to tell him what had been planned in passion while he was still a thousand miles away.

"Look, if you want me to see him—"

"I don't."

"If you want—"

"I don't, Hank. I don't!" My hands tightened on the sill. My eyes stayed fixed on the road, watching a car dip down from the highway and roll on toward the ranch, leaving a trail of dust that settled slowly in the hot air. "Someone's coming, Hank. You'd better get dressed."

"Let's get this straight. Let's—" His hands gripped my arms from behind.

"You better get dressed, Hank." I did not wait for an answer, but pulled away and walked out through the open doorway. I stood wearily on the porch, watching the car stop, watching Frieda climb down on her slim legs, wave, and rush toward me up the walk.

"Darling!" Frieda kissed me. She was laughing, jumping up and down like a child. Her eyes were bright and the excitement was all through her. "Here he is! Harry! My husband! He's back, he's back!" She left my side, rushed back to the car, and took the arm of her husband, who was moving toward us up the walk.

Harry Doyle was a j.g. in the naval air corps. He was boyish and pleasant and terribly in love with his wife. I saw it in the way he pressed Frieda's arm, in the way he looked down at her through his deep brown eyes, and the way he stood with his head cocked on one side, listening while she spoke. He shook my hand, said, "I've heard about you. Frieda keeps talking about you."

"Everything good, I hope."

"The best," he said, and followed us into the house.

Frieda explained they were on their way to Las Vegas to see Harry's family. They'd bought a second-hand car. Harry had a leave, and they were going to drive across the country, stopping in motels along the way. "A regular second honeymoon." And she laughed with the excited embarrassment of a bride.

Then Hank came out from the bedroom. He stood for a moment in the doorway, and Frieda's voice broke and her eyes widened and she said, "What the—what—?"

"Hank McKellar," I said. "I think you've met Hank."

"Yes, I—" Her eyes jerked to mine. I was looking at her steadily. I said, "Didn't Lloyd tell you?"

"Well, of course it was Lloyd who told me *you* were here. He got drunk, you see, and—But he didn't tell me—"

"He didn't know," I said.

"Neither did I. My God, neither did I." Frieda laughed nervously. She glanced at her husband and said, "Hank McKellar. A friend."

"Hank drops around every now and then," I said. "To help me exercise the horses."

"I love a good horse," Hank said. His voice was grim, but he managed a smile when he shook hands with Frieda's husband. Then he mixed the drinks. There was an awkward pause. Frieda looked from Hank to me, shook her red hair, murmured, "What do you know? What do you know?" Then finally she laughed, "Remember the last time I saw you, Martha? Remember all those months in that damned cottage? All those silly arguments and swimming and lying in the sun and cooking and waiting, and that awful boredom." She squeezed Harry's arm. "And you know whose fault it was. Yours, darling. You ran away and left me, so there was nothing to do but play bridge and argue."

Harry laughed. He said, "Well, it's harmless enough, anyway." He looked at me and said, "I'll bet she really got on your nerves sometimes. You know Frieda. Always has to be doing something, going somewhere. Boy, I'll bet she nearly went nuts with boredom!"

"Oh, I kept busy enough—what with all my men friends." And Frieda laughed, and we all laughed with her.

Then Hank brought the drinks. They were cold and good in the heat of the day. Frieda snuggled close to her husband on the sofa. They both looked very young sitting there together. They laughed a great deal, and Harry said, "By the way, baby, you know when I was helping you pack? Just before we left? Well, you know what I found in one of your drawers? A pair of men's nylon shorts, and there was one of those tags sewed inside, one of those laundry things, you know. It said, 'Major Kermit Mullins.'" He winked at me, screwed up his face in mock anger. "I demand an explanation!"

Frieda burst out laughing. "I told you I kept busy, honey." And she laughed some more, then looked at me and said, "You remember the major? Always coming around to go swimming on the beach, always using one of our rooms to change his clothes?" She laughed all the louder as though remembering. "And the time he got drunk and went swimming with his clothes on? I sent his wet things to the laundry for him, and he went back to camp in some of Lloyd's clothes, and he was so embarrassed he never came back again."

"Oh, he came back," I said.

"Oh—" A touch of shadow crossed Frieda's face. "Did he?"

"Yes, I understand he was in the Corsair for awhile. But after that embarrassing incident, he never did come back to the guest house again."

Frieda let her breath out slowly. There was silence, as heavy as the heat in the room. I rose and went quickly to the kitchen. I hated myself. I had purposely needled Frieda because suddenly now I resented her. Everything was going too well for her. There seemed to be no payments. Everyone was happy. No one was going to be hurt. I poured myself a large drink, followed it with a glass of cold water.

Frieda came in behind me. "Darling!" she said. "Was I surprised!"

"Were you?" I set the glass down carefully.

"But don't worry. You'd be amazed how everything will fall into place when Phil gets back. I mean it's just as if—"

"It isn't quite like that, Frieda."

But she paid no attention. It had been a certain way with her, and of course it was like that with everyone else too. "Everything right back where you left off. Really wonderful, Martha. And you know what the toughest part is? Getting rid of the guy. Not that Hank is anything like the major. I mean, you know—clinging and all that sort of thing. Not understanding, I mean. God, why can't men ever understand when something is *over*? Here your husband is back, so of course it's *over*, and well...." And she went on with exactly how difficult men could be.

I poured another drink. I kept my back to her and sipped at the liquor, looking out the kitchen window at the long rolling fields while Frieda talked on behind me.

"We were in his room at the Corsair, and we'd already ordered breakfast. I hadn't told him about Harry's coming back during the night, because why ruin our last night, you see? So I'd just gotten out of bed, and I said, 'My husband. Harry....'"

"What about Harry?" The major propped a pillow behind his head, lit a cigarette, and blew smoke into the hotel room.

"Nothing, except he's coming in this morning."

The major turned his head and stared at her. "This morning?"

"So I won't be seeing you any more, will I?" Frieda picked up her lipstick from the bedside table, painted her mouth carefully, and ran a wet tongue over her lips. Breakfast would be coming any minute now, and probably the wizened little bellboy would bring it. After that episode on Joan's bed there'd been no way out except to return to the Corsair for these morning breakfasts, and there was really no point in letting the bellboy embarrass her. Besides, she was quite justified in coming here now, since it wouldn't have been delicate to go back to the guest house with the major after Joan's death, and even besides that, this was the last time the bellboy would ever see her, anyway.

"Just like that," the major was saying while she brooded. "You make up your mouth and frown and think about something else and tell me your husband's coming. Then you pop out of bed, get dressed, wave goodbye, and that's the end of it."

"Well, of course we haven't had breakfast yet."

"No, of course you've got to say goodbye on a full stomach." He was angry, and Frieda looked at him, frowning. He really had no business being angry, and he was acting terribly childish about it besides. After all, she'd never said she was in love with him, and he'd never said he loved her, either. It was just that they seemed to get along so well together, and it was fun to have a big breakfast in bed instead of grubbing for toast around the guest house with Ellen and Colleen still there and—well, he was acting terribly silly about it. "After all," she pouted, "you're married too, aren't you?"

"What's that got to do with anything?"

"Well, you're not going to divorce your wife because of me, are you? I mean eventually you're going home and be a good husband, aren't you?"

The major didn't answer. He smoked and waited. Soon the breakfast arrived and the ancient bellboy arranged the tray on their laps, keeping his eyes on his work and his thoughts to himself. Then the major climbed out of bed in his nylon shorts and went into the bathroom.

Frieda watched the bellboy. She said, "You won't have to do this any more."

"Ma'am?"

"I won't be coming here any more."

He merely nodded, and she knew then that she should have kept her mouth shut and not tried to apologize or defend herself. She munched at a piece of melba toast and waited for the major to return.

Breakfast was awkward that morning. There was suddenly nothing to talk about. She wanted to tell the major about Harry, and about how funny it was the way she'd met Harry at that party in Las Vegas. But the major was not at all interested. He ground the toast between his teeth, complained that the eggs were cold, and finally lifted the tray from the bed and set it roughly on the floor. Then he leaned toward her and said, "All right, damn it, all right," and reached for the strap of her pink slip.

Frieda winced. She saw the angry look in the major's eyes and felt his rough hand on her shoulder. She pulled away. "You don't have to spoil it, you know." And she slipped out of bed and dressed carefully because there would not be time to change at the guest house before going down to San Diego for the reunion with Harry. She painted her mouth all over again, piled her red hair on her head, changed her mind, and brushed it down long behind her neck. All the time the major watched her, and he was still sitting there in his shorts, still glowering at her when she glanced at her watch and walked toward him across the room.

"It's been a lot of fun," she said. "You're really awfully nice, and maybe if you're around Las Vegas you can call me up and we can all have a drink together. You'd like Harry and—"

"To hell with Harry!"

"Well—anyway, you'd like him." She bent and kissed him soberly on his sunburned forehead. "Thanks for everything."

"Cut it out!"

"What?"

"Just cut it out!"

She raised her eyebrows, shrugged, then turned and walked to the door. "Anyway, it was nice," she said, and went out to the hallway and walked down to the elevator. Going down she let the major slip from her mind entirely, and there was Harry, taking the major's place. Sweet, wonderful Harry, who was really very young and understood the little things about her much better than the major had, or that lieutenant or that j.g. or any of the rest of them. And walking toward the bus stop, she wondered why she had ever seen anything in Major Kermit Mullins anyway. Sullen, grouchy, he never did understand. And that business of wanting her after breakfast just because he wouldn't see her again—it was disgusting really, and she ought to tell Harry about it because he'd understand perfectly, because Harry was very sensitive and—But of course she couldn't tell Harry about anything. It saddened her terribly. And all the way down to San Diego in the bus—all the way down she felt more depressed than she had in months....

"You see what I mean?" Frieda touched my arm.

I started and said, "Yes, yes, I see what you mean."

"Not that you can blame a man. I mean after all—"

"Yes," I said. "After all." And I went back to the living room.

Frieda and Harry left after another drink. "A long way to go," Harry said. He shook hands with Hank, while Frieda kissed me and whispered, "He's attractive though. I almost envy you." She winked and took Harry's arm. They waved and walked out to the sun and back to the car. They waved again and Frieda blew kisses and rested her head on her husband's shoulder as he swung the car around and drove back up the dusty road. Their laughter came out through the open windows. It followed them all the way.

"Well—" Hank was beside me. I turned, went back to the living room, picked up my half-empty glass, and drained it. He was watching me from the doorway. "I know what you're thinking."

"Do you?"

"That letter and now this. I know what you're thinking."

"I'm not thinking, Hank. I'm feeling." And the feeling was big and dangerous. Why not me? If it can happen like that with Frieda, why not with me too? I'm not at the end of any road. I haven't shut any door behind me. So it's an interlude. A love affair. Honest, at least, and something I wanted. But I'm not caught in it. Even at the last second, even then I could turn around and go back to Phil. Even at the very last second.

"You think you could do that?" It was as though he'd read my thoughts.

"What, Hank?"

"What Frieda did."

"She's in love with Harry."

He laughed, then dropped it. "Yes, I suppose she is."

"But there's a difference, of course. She doesn't *really* want anyone else." I watched him moving toward me. I stood quietly while he lifted me in his arms and sat on the sofa and held me close in his lap. I found myself trembling and heard his voice saying, "Nothing's ever fair, you know. You don't always get everything. Somebody gets hurt, and I'm a guy who really knows it." His voice was neither sympathetic nor understanding. He was telling me how you survived in his world. Not in anybody else's world. Only in his world.

I listened and felt that odd fear of him. It was a long time before the trembling stopped. I clung to him hard, almost in hatred, and I wished that somehow I could close and lock that open door in front of me.

CHAPTER SIXTEEN

OUR SECOND VISITOR arrived only three days later. It was early morning then. The knock sounded while I was in the kitchen making breakfast. Hank was still asleep, so I tightened the dressing robe around my waist, pushed sleepily through the living room, and opened the front door on a short, round little man with rimless glasses and a sunburned face. He wore a rumpled Palm Beach suit. His round belly rested on a large silver belt buckle. Behind him in the drive was a dirt-covered black business coupé.

The little man stood silent a moment, looking at me pleasantly through his pale eyes. Then he nodded and wiped his face carefully with a huge green handkerchief. "Mrs. McKellar?" he said. His voice was high. It squeaked.

"No, I'm afraid—"

"This is the property of Mr. Lloyd Watkins?"

"Yes. But you see—" I stumbled for some way to explain that I was not Mrs. Hank McKellar. I said, "I'm a friend of Mr. Watkins. I don't understand—" and I was still fumbling for words when the heavy crash sounded from the bedroom. We both started. The little man smiled and wiped his face again. I excused myself and went back to the bedroom, where Hank stood stiffly in the center of the rug. He wore blue cotton pajamas. Around him on the floor were the broken pieces of a china lamp. He clawed the sleep from his eyes and jerked toward me as I came through the doorway.

"Shut the door!" he snapped.

"What in the world—"

"Shut the door, I said!"

I shrugged, closed the door carefully, and leaned back against it. Hank had turned away. He was looking out the window at the dirty coupe. "Who is it?" he said into the glass.

"I don't know."

"He thought you were my wife."

"Yes."

"Did he ask for me!"

"No, I heard the crash and—"

"Was he *going* to ask for me!"

"I don't know, Hank. I've never seen him before, so I suppose he was really looking for—"

"Now listen!" He swung about, strode toward me, gripped my arms, and held me pressed back hard against the heavy door. "Get his name. Tell him you never heard of me. You're living here alone. You understand?"

"Yes, but I don't—"

"You don't have to see anything. Just do what I tell you."

"Hank—" I looked up to his face. His lips did not move when he spoke. His eyes were half closed, looking through me and beyond me to some other time I did not know. His hands were steel traps on my arms. "You're hurting me," I said.

"Sorry." He turned away and took off his pajama top. He flung it to the floor and began dressing hurriedly. "You better get back. Remember what I said." He spoke over his bare shoulder. I watched him and rubbed the pain from my arm. "Hurry up!" He crossed to the window sill, leaned there briefly looking out at the car in the drive.

I went back to the front doorway. The little man was slumped against the porch rail. He'd lighted a cigarette and the perspiration from his chunky hand soaked into the white paper. "Going to be a hot one," he said pleasantly.

"Yes...."

He sighed. "Something broke in there?"

"Yes, a lamp. It fell off the bed table."

"Well?" He pushed off from the rail and looked at me quizzically through his baby-blue eyes.

"I'm sorry, but you have the wrong place. There's no Hank McKellar here."

"I see." He shrugged, half turned, then looked back at me and smiled behind his glasses. "Did I say 'Hank McKellar?'"

"Yes, you—" And I stopped, remembering he'd said. "Mr. McKellar" and the word *Hank* had never been used. I blushed and talked rapidly, looking over his head at the morning dew on the grass behind him. I said I'd met a Hank McKellar at Lloyd Watkins' home. I said that since this was Mr. Watkins' ranch, I'd naturally assumed he was looking for that particular Mr. McKellar. I'd seen Mr. McKellar nearly a month ago, but hadn't laid eyes on him since. One word led to another, until the sentences tripped over each other and I let them all die away in the rising heat. "Well—" I said.

"Thank you, Mrs.—"

"Gwynn. Martha Gwynn. And you? I mean if I do run into Mr. McKellar?"

He hesitated, looking me up and down. "The name is Petey," he said finally. "I don't believe Mr. McKellar would know me. But if you do happen to see him, you might telephone me. Roger Petey. At the El Cortez."

"Yes, I'll—I'll let you know."

"You're very cooperative." He smiled again. But his eyes were everywhere. Over me and behind me and around me. "You're very kind." He bowed painfully, then turned and waddled off to the car, moving slowly in the increasing heat. He squeezed in behind the wheel, waved, and drove back up the road, leaving a long trail of dust behind him.

Hank was fully dressed when I returned to the bedroom. He was standing close to the door, and when I entered he slammed the door behind me, then flung it open again and strode out to the living room. He paced up and down, going nowhere, just walking around and around in the sunlit room. Then finally he stopped and said, "Look—my leave's up in two more days. We still haven't decided exactly what we're going to do."

"His name was Mr. Petey."

"All right. Petey. But we still haven't made any plans."

"No...."

"Well, I'm going to get an extension on my leave. Another thirty days. I think I can swing it all right, but it'll take a little time. A week. Maybe more."

"Hank—"

But he turned and strode back to the bedroom. He dragged his suitcase from the closet and started throwing in his clothes. "I'll go back to the ship today," he said over his shoulder. "I'll send a jeep out for you. Someone'll take you back to Lloyd's. Just stay there till I come for you."

"Hank, I don't understand—"

"I told you there's nothing to understand." His voice grated. He snapped the suitcase shut, and said it again, slowly and carefully. "I'm getting an extension on my leave. Somebody'll take you to the guest house, and I'll come for you in a few days. There's nothing else to—"

"I won't do it, Hank. I won't do it!" Somewhere inside me the trembling started. I was afraid then. I did not understand, and I felt the hysteria rising in my throat. "I won't do it! I won't, I won't!"

"You'll do it!"

"I won't!" I was screaming then. I tried to stifle my own voice, but it would not stop. I wanted Hank to hold me close and say quiet things and explain softly so that this hysteria would go away. But instead he stepped toward me and his hand swung up and smacked against my face. I stumbled backward, tripped on the rug, and sprawled out on the floor. My head rested back against the wall; my slippers were jerked from my feet. But the hysteria left me, so I only breathed heavily in astonishment and anger as I stared up at Hank's determined face.

He was standing over me. He spit out the words with his hands clenched into fists. "You don't get it, do you? Well, get this! I'm in love with you! That's why I smacked you! That's why you're going to do what I tell you! I'm in love with you, and there's nobody on earth going to keep me from having you." He was still talking when he knelt beside me. I expected apologies and tenderness. I expected a comforting kiss on my bruised cheek. But instead his hands were rough as they ripped open my dressing robe, cruel as they touched my body. His fingers dug hard into my back and his teeth bruised my lips.

I hated him. I tried to fight him off. But he held me down forcibly while his hands wandered over me, and I felt the passion rising inside me against my own will. When it was over, he stood abruptly and lifted me in his arms. He carried me to the bed and laid me down and pulled a sheet up to my chin. "I'm in love with you," he said quietly. "Don't forget that. Just—don't—ever—forget." Then he bent toward me again. I covered my face with my hands. But he drew the hands away, and kissed me very lightly on the bruised cheek. "I'm sorry," he said softly. "I'm a bastard and I'm sorry." They were the first really tender words he had ever spoken. It was the first time he had ever kissed me without that fierce intensity.

I lay quietly and watched him as he picked up his bag, walked to the door, and looked back at me with his face almost calm now. "I love you," he whispered. "That's all. I love you." Then he was gone, and a moment later, I heard old Walt's pickup truck stopping in the drive before the ranch. I heard Hank's voice say, "Let's go, Walt," and I heard the truck rattle off down the road.

Mrs. Mooney came over after lunch. "Hear your husband's left," she said. "Walt took him to the bus in the pickup."

"Yes, he's—he's trying to get an extension on his leave."

"Oh—coming back here, is he?"

"No, we're going somewhere else. A trip of some kind."

"Too bad."

"Why?" I looked up sharply.

"Nothin'. You seemed kind of happy here, that's all."

"Yes, we were happy." And I wondered if we had been. I decided we hadn't. We would never be happy anywhere. Hank was under my skin like an insidious cancer. He'd eaten away my moral values, my courage, my self-respect, all the faith I ever had in my own sense of balance. We might be together in the future, but somehow we would never be quite happy.

Mrs. Mooney left, and I packed slowly in the early afternoon. When I'd finished I rubbed cold cream on my bruised cheek, then sat in the living room and drank some of Lloyd's best brandy and kept my mind on little things—the ice in my glass, the starch that was slowly wilting from my dress. My emotions, however, were out of control. My arms still hurt where Hank had gripped them. Despite the cold cream, my face still hurt where he'd slapped it. My entire body ached from the fierce, possessive way he'd made love to me, and through all this and because of all this, I knew that I hated him and would not forgive him. Two more drinks made me more certain still. "I'm rid of you," I said aloud. "I'm finally rid of you." Then, standing to refill my glass, I remembered little Mr. Petey in his Palm Beach suit. I stood up and threw my glass into the fireplace. It made a beautiful sound, but did no good at all.

It was late afternoon when the jeep pulled up before the ranch. The driver was the young sailor from Tennessee whom I'd seen on Hank's ship on that very first night of all. He did not seem quite so young as he had in those weeks before. But sailors aged fast around San Diego.

Neither of us said anything. We nodded to each other, and he seemed embarrassed when he entered the bedroom for the bags. He carried them hurriedly to the jeep, then waited, smoking, while I said goodbye to Mr. and Mrs. Mooney. They both hated to see me go. They both said they hoped I'd come back with my husband some day. I said I would, and wondered if I might, and with whom, and if they would be there at that unknown time.

The young sailor had still not spoken when we started the fifty-mile drive to Salamanca. I was glad of the silence, and at the same time curious to know what he thought and what Hank had told him. I waited until we'd reached the hills over the valley—until the ranch was well out of sight. Then I glanced at his smooth round face in the mirror. "You know Mr. McKellar pretty well?" I asked tentatively.

He caught my eye, looked away. "Well," he said. "Well, he's helped me out a lot. Lent me the jeep and stuff."

"You like him?"

"Sure."

"He's a good officer?"

"Well—" He blushed a little, hesitated, then nodded yes. He did not like what I was asking, but could find no way to avoid my questions.

"Why did you hesitate?" I pushed him on unmercifully. "Why don't you want to answer?"

"Well, about being a good officer—I mean it depends on what you mean by a good officer."

"I see." I paused and wet my lips. I looked through the windshield at the passing mountains and wondered exactly what I did mean and exactly what I wanted to know. "You mean," I said finally, "you mean he's tough, don't you?"

The sailor was surprised. "How did you—"

"Oh, I know—I know."

"Well...." He softened a little then. "He ain't regular navy, you know. Merchant marine and—well, I seen him when we was in a small boat that run aground one time off Japan. Freezing water, and the only way to get afloat was climb out in the water and work her loose. So Mr. McKellar sends a couple of fellows over the side. They nearly froze to death. Afterwards one of 'em almost died of pneumonia. Anyway, this fellow in the water says something about why don't Mr. McKellar do it himself, and Mr. McKellar got sore and jumped over the side and let this fellow have it. Nearly killed him. Kept saying, 'Don't you ever say that to me again, don't you ever say that!' You know, almost crazy. So anyway, he got the boat loose and all, and when he got back to the ship the captain bawls him out for going over the side himself. 'You're in command,' the captain says. 'You're responsible for all those men, and you don't have to risk your neck by showin' off,' Well, Mr. McKellar just laughed. I never heard no one laugh so hard, and all the time he kept sayin', 'Gotta be the last to leave the boat. I'll remember that, Captain. Learned that already, Captain. Boat's just like a ship. Keep the boat afloat and be the last to leave it!' And then he just kept on laughin' till it sounded more like cryin' than anything else."

The boy paused. He glanced at me in the mirror. But I avoided his eyes. I said, "Is Mr. McKellar getting an extension on his leave?"

"We're sailin' in a couple of weeks."

"Oh?"

"So it couldn't be too long."

"No—it couldn't."

"He didn't tell me nothin' about a leave. Just telephoned me on the ship and said to go out and get you. Said—" He stopped.

"What did he say?"

"Said not to tell anyone he called. Said just to take you to Salamanca and bring along some of his gear and give it to you and not tell anyone."

"Some of his gear?" I said.

"Yeah. In the back there. A gun and some fishin' stuff. A few clothes. That's all." He laughed nervously. "I guess—I guess he *is* gettin' some extra leave after all."

"Yes," I said. "Yes, I guess he is."

We drove through town, up the gravel drive, and along the bluff to the guest house. The sailor helped me carry my own bags and Hank's few belongings into the cottage. It was empty, but I could see that Ellen still lived here, though of course Frieda had gone, and Colleen too, because her guitar and boots—everything—was gone from her room. I wondered where Colleen was. I thanked the sailor and watched him drive off fast along the bluff. Then I sat down on a bamboo chair and said, "Here I am again. Right back where I started." And God, how I wished it were really true!

CHAPTER SEVENTEEN

I N THE DAYS AFTER, I stayed close to the guest house. I waited in a positive, almost active way. But I was not the same person who had waited there in the months before. I was entirely unsure of what I waited for, and found no comfort whatsoever in the beach or the library or the games of cards that had formerly helped me pass away the hours.

Lloyd's house was quiet now. He gave fewer parties, and where once he'd been nervous, angry and superior, now he was completely resigned to that extreme loneliness that comes with the knowledge of one's own abnormality. He kept to the house as much as possible, carefully avoiding the possibility of running into stray sailors around the town, even ordering Koko to lock him in the house once he started drinking heavily. And he drank often over long periods of time. His once handsome face had gone to pieces in a matter of weeks. His hands shook. His pale eyes were red and watered. And yet as his body deteriorated with the alcohol that was with him all the time now, he became more pleasant, more understanding, more sympathetic than I had once thought possible. Lloyd Watkins was a thoroughly defeated man. Yet somehow now, in losing his pride of manhood, he had finally become a human being.

I know all this because I passed a lot of time with Lloyd in those days after I returned to Salamanca. Ellen had ceased going to his house entirely, and somehow I was drinking a great deal more now than I ever had before. It had begun at the ranch with

Hank, where liquor had seemed to be a normal part of our relationship. Now, with Hank gone, I found myself drinking alone,
feeling guilt because I wanted to drink. But the guilt was easily
eliminated—I called on Lloyd a great deal in order to convince
myself that I drank only to be sociable.

They were strange times, those afternoons and nights with
Lloyd. We sat across from each other in the big barren living
room. We talked a little of one thing or another while Koko served
the first two or three drinks on a small silver tray. The martinis
were mixed beautifully, poured gracefully, drunk slowly, as two
people tried hard to convince themselves they were enjoying two
harmless cocktails before dinner or before lunch, or just for the
hell of it in the middle of the morning. But after those first two,
Koko was always dismissed—casually but firmly with a "Thanks
just the same, Koko." Koko nodded. He locked the doors. He left
the bottle, the ice and a dozen clean glasses, and disappeared into
the far corner of the house.

Then we drank because we felt like it. We did not think
about drinking. We did not talk about it. And we no longer
spoke of common things. We talked of ourselves now. We
played Lloyd's jazz records—Bessie Smith and Bix Beiderbecke
and Jelly Roll Morton—and Lloyd bemoaned the loss of his
own physical desire for Ellen, the loss of his wife those ten years
before. He looked at me sadly through his bloodshot eyes and
said, "Funny about us. Disliked each other. Enemies. You the
nice young girl from New Hampshire, me the big rich bastard
who could have what he wanted. But we're on the same level
now. Same level." And he laughed and poured us both a fifth
cocktail and said, "The great equalizer, this stuff. The greatest
equalizer of all."

I nodded, but I never spoke of Hank. Lloyd knew, I think,
though perhaps he did not really understand. I went to Lloyd's

to pass time. I drank to pass time. I was not an alcoholic, and felt sure I never would be—if Hank returned soon enough.

And I used to think about that, wandering back to the guest house in the late of night, fighting my way through the trees, muttering the words sadly to myself. "Hate him ... bastard ... no good ... don't love ... but help me, help me ... need how strong you are...." And I'd laugh when I reached the empty living room—empty because only Ellen and I remained. Joan was dead; Frieda had gone off with her husband; Colleen had gone off somewhere by herself, gone to sing her songs, play her guitar in an unknown place. So I'd laugh alone. And I'd laugh the louder when Ellen came down the hall to meet me.

She had changed too. The jealousy was gone. The intense suspicion had left her. She was a thirtyish woman who had eventually discovered that it was quite possible to live without a man. It had surprised her. She had mellowed, and whereas before she had needed others but had defiantly lived within herself, now she needed no one and gave all of herself that anyone could ask.

"You shouldn't go over there," she'd say, making me black coffee, sitting across from me while I drank the bitter liquid with a shaking hand. "Lloyd's no good for you. Not that he's bad. But he's licked. And you're too young to be licked. You're just too damn young." Then she'd pause a moment. She'd smoke, and her dark round face would be almost benign, her voluptuous body almost motherly. "Funny," she'd say. "Funny. In the old days all I wanted was Lloyd. Now I think I'll settle for that chicken farm when my husband retires from the navy. I never did like chickens, but—" And she'd shrug and go down to the bedroom with me and sit heavily on Joan's empty bed while I undressed. She'd cross her legs and study me with her deep black eyes. "Where are you going, Martha?"

"Staying here, of course."

"I mean where are you *going?*"

"Don't know." I'd hang up my clothes, turn away, puzzled, avoiding the answer because I did not know any answer to this or anything else. "Just—going." And I'd flop naked into bed and sleep heavily until the next painful morning, the next endless day, the next comforting drink.

It was nearly three weeks in all. And in that time only two things came along to jar me from this timeless present of waiting for nothing but a miraculous escape from my own self-destruction. One was a letter from Phil. It was the most hopeful letter he'd written since he'd left me in the Mark Hopkins that million years ago. The end, he said, was actually in sight. He could not give any specific date, but it was absolutely definite that he'd be back very soon now. He hoped my waiting hadn't seemed too long. He hoped I'd found useful ways to occupy myself. We'd take a little vacation because he'd be released from the army then. He'd been in the Second World War and had been called back from the reserves for this tour of Korean duty. But this duty was ending, and there was no chance of his staying in the army unless there was another world war, which did not seem likely at the moment.

So we'd take a long vacation, then go to Sadler Falls for a visit with my family, then to Westchester, where we'd buy another, larger house. *Something in the twenty-five-thousand-dollar class,* he wrote. *Four shrubs instead of two. Three bedrooms and two baths. Martha and me and baby makes three—and everything will be better than ever.*

There was more. But I could not read it. I put my face down on the open letter and I cried in a way I had not cried since I'd been a very young girl and thought my heart was forever broken. Then finally, hours later, with a stiff drink to fortify myself,

I answered Phil's letter. One lie after another. It took me an hour and two more drinks to complete it.

Mr. Petey called on the following day. He wore the same Palm Beach suit, the same rimless glasses, the same quizzical smile. He came into the guest house and lowered his round body to the hassock. He took off his hat and his head was bald and glistening with perspiration. I watched him closely. He did not look like a very dangerous or even very dramatic man. He might have been a bill collector or a family friend of Hank's, who wanted to borrow money. He blew on his glasses and polished them carefully with his big green handkerchief.

"Seen Mr. McKellar lately?" holding the glasses up to the light.

"No...."

"Suppose you're wondering who I am."

"Naturally."

"Navy Department. Nothing very exciting." He smiled a little and perched the glasses across his pink nose. "Just going around checking on people. Strictly routine."

"Until you find something in the checking."

"Yes—until I find something." He frowned a little, stood up and hitched his trousers over his round stomach.

I turned away and tried to keep my voice casual. "Isn't Lieutenant McKellar attached to a ship? I mean, wouldn't he be on the ship and—"

"Among other things, Mr. McKellar has overstayed his leave."

"I see."

"Some of his gear was taken off." He paused a moment. "The ship sailed yesterday—without him." He stretched, waddled to the doorway and looked out at the calm sea. "We did find the sailor who took his gear from the ship. I believe he gave it to you. I believe the sailor even brought you here himself."

"Look," I said. "Look, Mr. Petey—"

"I just follow my orders, Mrs. Gwynn. I don't necessarily agree or disagree. Not much leeway for judgment."

"Would you believe me if I told you I didn't know where he is?"

"Tell me and I'll think about it."

"I don't know where he is. I don't know why you want him and I don't know where he is."

"I'll be back."

"I'm sorry I lied to you before. But—"

"But this time you can be quite honest because you don't know anything, anyway." He chuckled and turned from the doorway and said, "Sometimes you have to like a man. Maybe you even admire him. Maybe a woman could even love him. But war's a funny thing, Mrs. Gwynn. There's public feeling, you know. Might overlook that, and then you run into technicalities. Know what I mean?"

"No," I said. "I don't know what you mean." And I waited then, watching his calm, perspiring face. Every nerve in my body had tensed. I wanted to shake him, beat him, force out of him exactly what he was trying to say, why he wanted Hank, why Hank had deserted, where he thought Hank had gone. But Mr. Petey only shook his bald head slowly, put on his hat, and turned and puffed out along the bluff and back through the trees to his waiting car.

After he'd gone, I mixed myself a very stiff drink, then sat at the dinette table, where I'd drunk coffee in the weeks before. I thought that really I liked coffee better than liquor, so why not have coffee now? It was a fine, moral idea. I carried the drink to the kitchen and deliberately poured it down the drain. But then, watching the cold brown liquid flow across the white enamel, I changed my mind. I did not want coffee after all. So I made another drink and sat on the sofa because I'd never sat on the sofa while drinking coffee. I would not think of coffee again.

I thought about Mr. Petey. I thought about Hank. It was odd that I'd spent these past two weeks waiting for something to happen without ever considering what that something might be. I'd known all along that whatever it was, it would undoubtedly be the biggest step I'd ever taken and would surely change my entire life. Yet somehow I had not wanted to make any decision. Since the moment I'd let my guard down with Hank McKellar, Hank and Fate had pretty well taken care of every move I'd made. I had not liked those moves, and yet I had never resisted. The moving finger had written and moved on, and I was content to become completely apathetic, letting the finger keep writing the way it liked.

I took a long swallow and set the glass down hard on the wicker table. I'd make a stand, that's what I'd do. I'd stop this wavering between a physical desire for Hank and a sentimental memory of Phil. I'd stay right here and I'd stop drinking. And when and if Hank came for me, as he'd said he would, then I'd tell him the whole affair was over, ended, done with. He'd kept things from me. He'd treated me with little respect and no consideration. Certainly. I'd been weak and certainly I was to blame. But beginning right now—right this second—all this was going to change. Little old Martha Gwynn was going to be reborn. She was going to forget, go back to being the innocent little girl from Sadler Falls, go back to being the little housewife in a Westchester housing development. She was going to wait for Phil and she was going to quit drinking.

I'd already finished half the drink, so my courage had blown up like a balloon inside me. "Right now!" I said aloud. "To hell with you, Hank McKellar! To hell with you, 100-proof bourbon!

To hell with all of it!" I stood and posed dramatically. This was the big moment.

Then, as the future loomed almost visible and almost beautiful before me, two figures appeared in the open doorway. They were both girls, both about my age, and yet somehow ages younger than myself. They understood there were vacancies in the guest house. A friend of Mr. Watkins had arranged for them to stay here if they liked. And Lord, they could think of nothing better! "With that beautiful beach ... and our own cottage ... all of us working together ... why the time will pass so quickly ... just heaven ... just absolute heaven!" They went on with enthusiasm bubbling all through them.

"Wonderful," I said. "Yes, it's absolutely wonderful." I kept saying it over and over as I followed them about while they inspected the cottage. When they left they promised to bring over their clothes within the next few days. I stood in the doorway and watched them dance like young children across the lawn. "There I went," I thought. "There went Martha Gwynn." And after they'd disappeared from sight, I turned back to the empty room. I tried to assume my pose of bravado. "To hell with Hank!" I said. But somehow the words lacked conviction. "To hell with 100-proof bourbon!" But at some time or other in those past few minutes, I'd already drained the glass to the bottom.

There was no point in flinging an empty glass. Might as well refill it.

CHAPTER EIGHTEEN

FIRST SAW THE blue sedan from beneath the portico that hung across Lloyd's gravel drive. But night was fighting its way across the sky, and after those five martinis one blue sedan more or less made little difference. I looked back at Lloyd who teetered in the doorway. I said goodnight, "See you 'morrow," and I pulled myself together and forced my legs to move in a straight line across the gravel. "Blue sedan," I told myself, and wavered on through the trees, feeling the night coming down like a great tent above my head. I thought that I'd gone to Lloyd's for one martini and Lloyd hadn't been at all fair to make such a large pitcherful. You make a drink, you drink a drink. You make a big pitcherful, you let it stand, and the ice melts. Makes it taste bad. All wrong to let it stand. All wrong for Lloyd to mix up so many.

I shook my head, trying to shake away the buzz in my ears and the film behind my eyes, then gave it up, knowing from experience that only sleep was of any use at all. So, crossing the living room, I was headed directly for my bed. There was nothing else in my mind until I'd reached the bedroom doorway—where I stopped abruptly and looked straight into the gray eyes of Hank McKellar. He'd gotten my suitcase down from the closet and was throwing my clothes into it without even bothering to fold them. He looked at me grimly and said, "I told you I'd be back. I told you to be ready."

"Rumpling my clothes."

"You're drunk."

"Not so very drunk."

"Tight." He was disgusted. He turned away and slammed the suitcase shut.

"All right," I said indignantly. "All right." I slumped at my small desk and watched him. He did not look at me. He kept on packing a second suitcase with a fury that made me sense I should say nothing. He was running this show, and there was nothing I could do about it. I turned away and stared down at the desk. There was an empty envelope lying torn in one corner. I picked it up idly. It was the opened envelope from one of Phil's letters.

Hank was watching me. He frowned. "Let's go."

"Got a letter here." I studied the envelope with that meaningless concentration of one who's been drinking and tries to convince himself he doesn't feel it. "Little old letter from little old husband in Korea. Just came. Today."

"All right! Come on!"

"Don't remember," I said. "Postmark—today. Don't remember." Then I sat motionless a moment, staring at the postmark and the writing, trying to remember what that letter had said, when I had read it, what it had said. But it was no good. "Can't remember," I said again. "Just can't—"

"Come on!" Hank gripped my arm as I babbled on. He half lifted me from the chair, pushed a purse into my hand, and still holding me firmly, led me out of the house and across the bluff. He carried two suitcases and the equipment that had been left with me by the young sailor. At the swimming pool he stopped, rested, and shifted the luggage to the other hand. I sat down and watched him through the darkness. The envelope was still clutched in my fist. I pushed it into my purse and asked myself who this Hank McKellar was to go around packing my bags and kidnapping me right out of Lloyd's guest house. "Who are you, anyway?" I said. "Who do you think—"

"Never mind that."

"Where we going?"

"Come on!"

"Won't! I won't!"

"You're tight, and you will!" His strong hand pulled me up and half carried me though the trees to the blue sedan. He put the bags in back, pushed me into the front seat, climbed in beside me, and raced off down the drive. "I got the car yesterday," he said. "It's a junk, but it'll get us there."

"Where's it getting us?"

He did not answer. And even with my mind confused and clouded, I understood exactly why he refused to explain. He wanted to tell me, but did not think I could possibly understand. If he'd found me completely sober, we might have argued and I might have won. But I hadn't been sober, and Hank was making my mind up for me in the way he thought I wanted it. I understood this in the back of my mind. Yet I could not find the effort to put it into words, did not have the will to resist Hank's determined anger.

We drove fast down the highway. I recognized the outskirts of San Diego. We passed the naval base, where the ships were black silhouettes against the sky, where in daytime, pelicans stood knee deep in the shallow water along the shore. "You deserted," I said accusingly. "Mr. Petey told me."

"You've seen Mr. Petey again?"

"Nice man. Fat little man."

Hank laughed. He pressed down on the accelerator and drove on past the naval base, heading straight for the Mexican border. Night was on us. I was hungry. I wanted a drink. The martinis were wearing off and a headache was coming and my mouth was dry. "Go to sleep," Hank said.

"Won't go to sleep." Yet my head fell forward and I dozed, conscious of the smooth highway changing to a bumpy road, conscious of the car's stopping and of Hank's voice making hurried explanations to a man with a Spanish accent. Someone opened the trunk. Someone looked in the back seat and rummaged through our luggage. Then we were moving again, more slowly now, until the lights of a town knifed under my half-closed eyelids, until we stopped and a Mexican bellboy opened the car door and took out the bags.

"All right," Hank said. "We're staying here for the night." He held my arm as we crossed a dusty street and entered the dingy lobby of a small hotel. "We're in Tiajuana. The Hosteria del Sol."

"The Hosteria del Sol," I repeated. "What do you know? About a month too late."

"What does that mean?"

"Started down here once with Lloyd and the girls. Never got here. Running away from you then. And here we are together." I laughed foolishly. "Rotten little hotel."

"We'll only be here one night." He led me on through the lobby into the adjoining bar. He pulled out a chair, pushed me down behind the chromium table. He nodded to a waiter who brought pink tequila sunrises, and he watched me as I drank mine fast. I felt my head clearing until finally I was fully awake and almost completely sober. The room was dark and dirty. A number of sailors stood at the long bar, drinking fast, looking at their watches, glancing at me between gulps of whisky. Hank still watched me closely. And now for the first time I saw him in some reasonable focus. He wore civilian clothes—flannel slacks, a rather loud sport coat, a blue sport shirt open at the collar. He ordered a second tequila sunrise, let me finish, then beckoned to the waiter, who brought me a large bowl of chili. It was very hot, but there was a bottle of beer too, so I kept most of the nausea down along with the food.

"You do this often?" Hank dropped his eyes and drummed his fingers on the table. "Get tight like this?"

"I thought you liked to drink."

"Drink. Not get drunk."

"You're so tough, Hank. You're so real real tough."

He bit down on his lip. "Maybe it's better this way. It saved any arguments."

I laughed and remembered that I had wanted to resist him. I tried to force the anger into my throat, but it would not come. I felt sick. My face was hot, my stomach fluttering. "Tough," I said again. "Tough." And I studied the word *Cerveza* on the bottle of beer, then poured out the last foaming drop, drained the glass, stood, and walked through the tables to the ladies' room. It was a small, dirty closet. I sat on the cracked toilet cover and smoked, and from outside I could hear the incongruous music of a cowboy song played on a guitar. I started, then stood, finished the cigarette, and extinguished it under the leaking faucet. I washed my face, put fresh lipstick on my mouth, and studying my own face, I thought I'd better not have any more to drink. I wondered what I was doing down here in Tiajuana with Lieutenant Hank McKellar. I wondered what I felt about all this, and I wondered why I kept hearing that guitar music through the thin walls of this Mexican cafe.

A good five minutes passed before I shuffled back to the table. During that time I sat once more on the closed toilet seat and listened dumbly to the guitar that was accompanied now by a harsh, twangy voice. Finally I shook my head and moved slowly into the smoke-filled room. I sat at the table, peered over the tables at the singing girl, smiled ironically to myself, and nodded to Hank. "Remember her?"

"Sure. At Lloyd's party."

"Colleen Sims." I laughed. "Funny. Sure funny." And I watched Colleen through the swirling smoke that hung like a blue fog in the rays of the spotlight on her body. She was dressed in boots, shorts and a cowgirl vest, designed to expose as much of her angular body as the cafe thought allowable. On her head was a ridiculous ten-gallon hat. She stood stiffly by the microphone, strumming the guitar in a horribly mechanical way, while she sang in that hoarse voice, that colorless voice I'd heard from the ladies' room. Once, back there in the naval hospital— back then when she'd been entertaining a legless marine private named Paul Sarkis—Colleen's voice had contained a freshness, an enthusiasm that made up for what it lacked in quality. Now even youth was gone. She was an older, discouraged girl, singing for drunken sailors who told dirty jokes during the music and clapped only in appreciation of her scanty costume.

I did not want Colleen to know I'd seen her act. So I waited until she'd bowed out through the scattered applause. Then I fought through the smoke once more, pushed open the plywood door to her dressing room—a tiny, filthy little place with a board for a table and one jagged piece of broken glass for a mirror.

She showed no surprise at seeing me. She grinned through the badly applied grease paint. She said, "Hello, Martha Gwynn," laughed, and took a large swallow from a bottle of Mexican rum on the crude table before her. "Have some?"

"Thank you." I lifted the half-filled bottle. I told myself I didn't want any rum. I was doing this to keep from hurting Colleen's feelings. But the rum felt good inside me all the same. I set the bottle down on the floor, coughed and said, "Fine. Very fine!" Colleen grunted. I coughed again. And then for a moment we merely looked at each other with an unspoken sadness there between us.

"See my act?" Colleen said finally, not looking at me.

"No...."

"You're lucky." She seemed relieved. She laughed again and said, "On the other hand, it's practically your last chance. I'm through this week. Quitting. Going back to Oklahoma. Husband's coming in, so I'm going home and live right and get in shape to meet him."

"I'm glad, Colleen—about his coming back."

"Sure—he'll open another hardware store. Fail again probably. But I don't know—there's all kinds of failures. Failing in hardware doesn't seem quite so bad, any more."

"I know. Sure, I know."

"Do you?"

"Yes, I think I know."

"When I used to go to the hospital, it felt different. I was doing something. Or maybe I wasn't. Maybe that fat nurse had the right idea. Sleep with these guys. I guess that's about all you *can* do for them."

"Colleen...."

"Oh, I didn't used to think so. Maybe I still don't, not underneath. You see, I've—I've tried it. Right here. Upstairs in one of the hotel rooms. A very nice and very handsome sailor. Last night before sailing and all, but—you know what he did? Gave me five dollars. I don't know—I just stood there looking at the money. I wanted to throw it in his face. But he wouldn't have understood, so I didn't and—maybe it was better that way. Maybe—" She stopped, took another swig of rum, but this time did not offer one to me. She was getting morose, and I felt perhaps it had been a mistake to see her. Perhaps I reminded her of a better time.

I stood up. "Well—I'm glad it's almost over."

"How about you? Who you with?"

"Hank McKellar. You met him that night at Lloyd's party."

"Sure, I remember."

"You know about it, don't you?"

"Right after you left, Lloyd got drunk. He talked to everyone."

"Well...." There was nothing more to explain, no more past between us. I said it again. "Well...." and saw her watching me, shaking her head.

"You're the last one, Martha. Those wives—they come and go. But I always thought you'd stick it out. Strongest, most normal. And now—"

"Now?"

"Nothing. I'll see you." She stood and we shook hands. It was an awkward moment. Everything had been mentioned. Nothing had been said.

"Good luck," I murmured. And I turned and left her there in the filthy little room. I went back to the chromium table and ordered rum. I drank it quickly.

Hank watched me. "Martinis," he said. "Then beer, then rum. You'll feel like hell tomorrow."

"Don't forget the tequila."

"Feeling nasty, aren't you?"

"A little."

"Ever see me nasty?"

"Lots of times."

"I mean *really* nasty. Ever see me when someone tried to break up what I wanted and what I believed in?" He was staring at me with his eyes in little points. "Your husband, for instance. Ever think what I'd do to hold onto you? Keep us together? Ever think how far I'd go?"

"I can guess." I tried to laugh it off, but his eyes were still narrowed, still watching me. "Hank," I said. "You're a bastard. A real bastard."

"You don't mean that." He was smiling.

"Don't I? Don't I?"

"Come on!" He gripped my arm, pulled me up from the table, led me out to the lobby and up in the shaky elevator to our room. It was dark and shabby. The dirty curtains hung limp in the dust-filled air that dragged itself over the window sill. Hank flicked on a bed lamp, then pushed me down on the bed. He held me there while he stood over me, his mouth twitching, his fingers digging into my arms. "It's been a couple of weeks now, hasn't it, baby? But I'm not trying anything when you're tight."

I laughed nastily. "Remember that first night? Down on the beach?"

"That was *your* idea—and you were sober."

"Yes—Yes, I was." I felt ashamed. "A long time ago," I whispered. "Long time ago." And I rolled over on the bed and lay quiet while Hank removed my shoes. He was careful not to touch me again. He did not even remove my dress. I lay there with my eyes closed, my head swimming, wondering if this were the very room in which Colleen had received her five-dollar bill, trying to forget Colleen, remembering the long time ago on the beach and the longer time ago before that—and the longest time ago of all, back there in Sadler Falls, New Hampshire. And it was pleasant to see it now, and to hear it now and be there in Sadler Falls, New Hampshire. The bright sun was there in Sadler Falls. The way it came up in the morning, and all the spider webs on the green grass, disappearing slowly when the heat first came. And the way the heat lay over the fields and seemed to wiggle in the summer time, rising up like steam. The crickets so hot and tired they could hardly chirp; and those big black and yellow spiders that climbed on blackberry bushes. All the leaves turning in the fall, and the hound dogs calling from way down in the woods. And the Christmas-like postcards, and the hunters with their checkered shirts and laced boots, and big setter dogs. The way it felt to walk bare-footed in the grass, in the early morning when the ground was wet. And the loons screaming down on the river, and the stars so close you could touch them if you stood on tiptoe. If you stood very high, reached very high, stared very hard out there somewhere—out there somewhere—

Out there somewhere a guitar was playing. Out there some-where a voice said, "Wouldn't touch you when you're tight." Out there somewhere was a very nice, very normal girl who never got tight and never let anyone touch her. Martha Gwynn was out there somewhere. I tried to find her, but she was gone in the red, blinking lights that consumed my brain.

CHAPTER NINETEEN

A FAT, BLUE-WINGED FLY walked on the cracked ceiling. It paused to rub its hairy legs together, buzzed, then flew away. There was a purple haze where the blue fly had been. Inside the haze was PAIN. It was an object I could see, touch, actually smell, there in the purple haze.

I groaned and struggled to a sitting position. Finally I stood and hung onto the bed, then supported myself on the wall during the agonizing struggle to the bathroom, where I splashed water on my face and saw the blinding pain once more, visible now in the face that leered at me from the bathroom mirror. The eyes in the face were red-rimmed with black moons beneath them. The mouth twitched. The tongue was swollen. I groaned, "Oh, God! Oh, God, oh, God!" and wanted to scream, with the knives inside me.

Hank was still asleep when I returned to the bedroom. He looked older, exhausted, like a man in a foxhole sleeping lightly, with a gun beside him. But I could not afford to be sorry for Hank now. I dressed and moved painfully to the hallway, closing the door soundlessly behind me. The elevator operator smiled at me with white protruding teeth. "Tequila," he said. "Bad in morning. Tequila." He laughed and closed the doors of the iron cage.

There was no sun over Tiajuana. The streets were quiet except for the naked, hairless dogs, and the cats that crept from nowhere to stare at me with yellow eyes. But there was a fruit stand on the corner. I bought two bananas and an orange, ate them slowly, leaning against the stand under the red-striped awning. I looked out at the dirty street and the gray haze above the town. But the pain would not diminish. My head was a glass bowl that would break if I turned it sharply. I struggled back down the street, stopping often to lean against a building and pull myself together for another few agonizing steps. It was nearly ten when I reached the hotel once more and sprawled exhausted in a wicker chair in the dingy lobby. My head was splitting. Great butterflies fluttered in my stomach. I closed my eyes tight, then opened them sharply, and for a second the pain was gone. But it came sliding back immediately, bringing hammers that drummed inside my head.

People passed indolently across the lobby. I watched them through half-closed eyes. Sailors, prostitutes, tourists who'd come for the races and the bull fights. I shut my eyes again, dozed, opened them slowly on the figure of a round little man in a Palm Beach suit. He might have been watching me. He might have been smiling. He might have been Mr. Petey.

I did not know. I had neither the moral will nor the physical strength to move away from him or toward him or any way at all. Yet sprawled there in the wicker chair with my eyes half closed and the drums inside my head, I caught myself hoping that it was Mr. Petey after all. If it were, then perhaps everything was not entirely lost.

Minutes later, Hank came down in the elevator with our bags. He grinned at me and said, "I told you you'd have a tough morning. Want some breakfast?"

"No, thanks."

"Well, then, let's go." And he took my arm, gently now, and led me out along the hot, dusty street to the blue sedan.

We drove out of town, going southwest. The road was narrow, filled with ruts. Cattle blocked our way, and once a

Mexican farmer kept his burro stubbornly in the center of the road, ignoring Hank's curses and the harsh shrieking of the horn. Hank drove straight through, nudging the burro aside with the fender.

"Just a few hours' drive," he said as we bumped along. "A fishing town called Capoca. I've bought a boat down here." He smiled with his thin mouth. "Told you we'd go off on a boat some day."

I did not answer. I watched Hank's face in the car mirror. It was a good-looking face. Lean, tan, attractive. Yet it was a face I did not recognize. Grinning, yet wild, with a half-crazy look around the eyes. Hank had always been intense and quick-tempered. But this was more—the face of a man who has decided what he thinks, what he believes, what he is going to do, a man who can smile because he knows finally that he will not be changed or stopped by anyone.

"Hank—" I stared ahead at the brown rutted road.

"What?"

"You know, back there in the hotel?"

"What about it?"

"Well—" I stopped, I'd been about to mention Mr. Petey. But remembering Hank's face, I realized for the second time that I wanted Mr. Petey close. Somehow I was frightened and somehow I relied on Mr. Petey.

We drove on, and my head cleared slowly so that I could think and try to pull things into perspective. But nothing made any sense. I was here with Hank McKellar because I'd been drinking all day yesterday, because I'd had a hangover all morning. It had been quite a while since I'd wanted Hank in any positive way. There'd been no good moment between us since we'd left the ranch. So I was with him now because of circumstances, because we were partners in sin, because we had said we wanted each other, and after destroying my entire former life to have him, I hated to admit that either of us could ever have been wrong.

We stopped for lunch at a small café along the roadside. We drank wine and ate tortillas, and Hank relaxed even more. He even smiled, and even touched my hand across the wooden table. He even pushed a touch of tenderness into his awkward words. "I know, baby. It's tough. You don't know what's going on with me, and I've been a real bastard about the whole deal. But believe me, it's for us. You weren't feeling good yesterday, so I had to think and act for both of us, and—well, I always told you it would work out. And it will. I promise you it will."

"All right, Hank." I looked at the purple liquid in my glass. The wine had settled my stomach. I felt tired, but a great deal better than I had in forty-eight hours. I watched Hank's calm face and groped for straws. "Maybe," I said softly, "if you told me all about yourself."

"I will."

"I mean now."

He frowned a little. "Look, I've bought a boat, Martha. Not much, but enough to get away on. We'll ease along down the coast, stop off here and there, really get to know each other. You can get a Mexican divorce, so there won't be anyone between us. We'll get on the boat. Maybe a month, maybe two months. I'll tell you all about myself then. We'll see this divorce thing through and we'll get married—and—and then I'll go back and see this Mr. Petey. I'll look him up myself. Get it straightened out."

"The criminal turns himself in."

"I'm not a criminal, baby. But I can't explain it to you now because right now—right now I don't think you'd believe me."

"No, I—I don't think I would." I hated to say it, but it was true—I wouldn't have believed him.

"You see?" There was pain behind his eyes. He lifted his wine glass, then set it down again; and for the first time since I'd known him, I saw Hank McKellar with his guard down. I'd thought Hank could never be hurt by anyone. Now I realized that he could—hurt, destroyed, driven to desertion, flight and a willingness to fight the world by himself. And all because of me. Martha Gwynn. Me.

I glanced at his face once more. His eyes were begging. "Do you love me?" they said. And then, "Please love me." And then the fire returned and the eyes said, "I'll make you love me! I'll beat you into loving me!" I pulled my own eyes away. I laughed and stood and felt his tall body behind me as we walked out to the car and the dusty road that was splattered now with the first few drops of rain.

The rain fell in black rods as we drove into Capoca. The streets were turning to mud, and the gray sea was a dead calm, broken only by the machine-gun drops of the rain itself.

"Not much of a town," Hank said, "but the boat's sound enough." He leaned forward to see through the mud-splattered windshield, and he did not speak again as we bounced through the ruts, sucking up mud that made a whooshing noise after the wheels were back on firmer ground.

Hank was right. Capoca was not much of a town. There was only one building over two stories high, and even that was made of drab, cracked adobe that blended perfectly with the dark brown streets. A few fruit and vegetable stands, a drug store, and a barbershop were about the only stores in sight. The two-story hotel boasted a red neon light that was turned on now in the late afternoon. *Hotel* it read, with half the *e* missing.

Hank parked near one of the five rickety docks, where unpainted fishing boats were tied side by side like docks in themselves. He took our bags, his .45 revolver, and his fishing gear from the car, and strode fast along the pier. I followed with the rain soaking through to my skin, plastering my clothes against my shivering body. Hank called back over his shoulder, "Get provisions tomorrow ! Then we'll sail right away! Leave the car here and dock here again when we come back!"

I did not answer. I raised my eyes from the rotted boards beneath my feet. Hank was walking with his body bent forward. There was a kind of triumph in the way he lunged into the rain. "He's crazy," I thought then. "Look at the way he walks. Listen to the things he says. He's crazy. Out of his mind." Yet I followed him all the same. It was raining harder than ever. There was nowhere else to go.

The boat looked very small. "Thirty-two feet," Hank said, and laughed as he helped me down to the slippery deck. "A sloop. No engine. But don't worry, I've been sailing all my life." And he flung open the hatch and descended before me to the cabin below. There were three bunks, a head, a sterno stove. The pots and pans were greasy, the blankets torn. Hank said the important thing was the hull and rigging. They were sound enough, and he'd done a lot of work himself during that two weeks I'd been waiting in the guest house. "We'll clean up in here after we get out to sea. I hate it as much as you do, but let's get out of here first. Let's get out of here! Let's get *out* of here!" His voice rose, then broke abruptly. He sat down on one of the bunks and looked at me slowly. "Afraid there hasn't been much time to talk. But tonight—I'll rustle up something to eat. You can dry off and watch me."

"I'm cold, Hank."

"Wrap up in some blankets."

"I'd like a drink."

He turned from the stove where he was opening a can of beans. He said nothing, but lit a kerosene lamp and dropped the match carefully into the sink. "Baby, we're getting back where we were for a while there at the ranch. It was the only right time in my life, and we're getting it back if I have to kill us both to do it."

"Just because I'm cold. That's all. I'm cold."

"Well—" He shrugged and drew a bottle from his open suitcase. It was bourbon. He poured a thimbleful into a tin cup and watched me drink it, then had a double shot himself.

I laughed ironically. "You're wrong about one thing, Hank. I don't need liquor any more than you do. It isn't me that needs it. Never was and never will be."

"So?"

"You don't need it, either. Us. We need it. Without it we haven't got anything at all. With it—" I paused. It had occurred to me that with it we had nothing either.

"Maybe," Hank said. "But we're only taking a couple of bottles with us anyway. We'll find out how much we need it."

I thought of that single night on the ranch when we'd gone an entire evening without a drink. I remembered how bored we'd been with each other, how little we'd found to say, how we could not even make love. But I said nothing. I undressed and wrapped myself in a blanket while Hank finished cooking the supper of beans and bread and black coffee. We ate, each in a bunk, sitting across from each other, with the kerosene lamp swinging above our heads. I kept the blanket tight around my naked shoulders, not only from cold, but from a new modesty, too.

It was quite late when we finished eating. Hank rinsed out the pottery dishes, then went up on deck. He was gone for some time, so I slipped into one of the bunks and lay there smoking, listening to the rain pounding heavily on the roof. If I turned my head sideways I could see the bottle of bourbon protruding from the clothes in Hank's open suitcase. It would be terribly easy to reach out and take a very large drink. But my hand did not move, and for a while I lay there puzzled, wondering why I did not even *want* to drink, though underneath I suppose I really knew. At the ranch I had drunk because Hank and I were together and drinks seemed to make that togetherness even more intimate. Then, at Lloyd's, I had drunk to keep my feelings for Hank alive in his absence. We'd met over a cocktail and we'd existed over highballs. Somehow I'd thought that a few drinks could keep us going forever.

In a way it was good to know this. On the other hand, it meant the end of something. I thought about it for a long time. Then I sat up in the bunk and bent forward over Hank's suitcase. I picked up the bottle, shook it, and put it down again. It meant nothing to me. Nothing at all. I started to laugh, pushing the bottle back under his clothes. And it was then, with my fingers in his suit case, that I found the letter. I recognized the writing immediately. Phil's. And immediately I remembered that empty envelope I'd found on my desk only two days before, when I'd come upon Hank packing my bags in the guest house. Hank had opened a letter from Phil. He'd kept it, and here in his open suitcase was the letter.

I despised Hank McKellar. My mind and emotions tried to concentrate on what Phil had written. But I could not grasp the words. I could not make sense from the sentences. I understood only one thing—the over-all content, the over-all message—Phil had flown out of Korea. According to the date on the first page of the letter, he was already back in the United States.

I do not remember exactly what I did after that knowledge had become a part of me. I know I stuffed the letter into my purse. I know I picked up the bottle once more and took a very long drink with a shaking hand. Suddenly the falling rain sounded like cannon balls on the deck above. I know I fell back in the bunk and wrapped myself even tighter in the torn blanket. I know my eyes found the gently swinging kerosene lamp and focused on the flickering light, fascinated with the rhythmic motion. Suddenly the hatch slid open and Hank's legs appeared on the tiny ladder.

He was soaking wet. He glanced at me, then undressed and dried himself hard with an old towel. I watched him without speaking. He hung the towel over the wash basin, drew a little water into the tin cup, and approached his open suitcase. He frowned, then lifted the bottle and held it up carefully to the kerosene lamp. Now, with the light behind it, I could see the scratch he'd made on the label before he'd left. The whisky was a half-inch below the mark. He poured himself a drink, then turned very slowly and said, "I ought to sock you one."

I did not answer.

"I can't leave for five minutes. You've got to have a drink."

"I don't want a drink, Hank."

"You took one."

"I didn't want one."

"I see. You needed one. You're cold." His voice was ironic.

"No, I wasn't cold."

"Your God damned nerves, I suppose."

"Yes, Hank, my nerves."

He laughed nastily and stuffed the bottle back in the suitcase. But his hand remained firm on the bottle's neck. His body hunched forward and his eyes looked carefully at the clothes. His fingers picked up a shirt, lifted it clear, then put it back again. He knew I was watching him. He turned away and I saw his eyes swing to the suitcase, then moved back slowly to my face. "All right," he said.

"I can't help my nerves."

He stared at me, and he must have been trying to read my eyes—either I hadn't found the letter, or I had and was going to say nothing about it. He had his reasons for saying nothing; I had mine. Any argument now would only serve to increase that crazy determination I'd seen mounting steadily during the past two days. The idea now was to keep Hank as calm as possible until tomorrow.

"I'm tired," I said as casually as possible. "Goodnight, Hank."

He watched me a moment with his eyes narrowed. Then he grunted and blew out the kerosene light. I turned my face toward the inside of the bunk and waited. I heard him sit down on his bunk. I heard the cigarette sizzle as he rose and tossed it in the sink. Then, after a long time, I heard his voice very close to my ear. "Martha—"

I stiffened and kept my lips clamped tight together.

"Want me to tell you why we're here? Everything? Want me to tell you now?" His hand touched the blanket, ran over its surface and under it until he had found me. His fingers were cold, touching my back and shoulders.

My muscles stiffened. His fingers paused, then slid carefully away. His body thumped into his bunk, and there was deadly silence from inside the cabin.

Outside the rain made a steady roar on the deck above.

CHAPTER TWENTY

WHEN I AWOKE there was daylight outside the porthole. My watch showed ten after ten, and Hank's bunk was empty. But there was coffee on the stove, and I drank three cups and smoked three cigarettes. Then I dressed and went up on deck. The rain had stopped, though a wind had risen; and the fishing boats thumped against the rubber tire fenders that kept them separated. Hank was nowhere in sight. But leather-faced fishermen wandered by on the pier. They looked at me and jabbered in Spanish. Some of them laughed.

I laughed back at them. I knew—all night I'd known—exactly what I was going to do. Phil was back in the United States. I didn't know where, nor how I'd find him. But I would. I'd do exactly as I'd told Hank I would during those better days at the ranch. I'd explain everything, and then, with my mind finally clear, I'd start a life somewhere, somehow—but not with Hank McKellar. Because things had changed since those days on the ranch. The fire had gone out of my desire. And now, with Phil back, all those plans we'd made seemed very unreal and very far away—just as Phil had seemed far away only hours before.

The idea that I would, that I actually *could* leave Hank McKellar seemed almost unbelievable. It meant a great many things. It meant no more drinking, no more confusion, no more passion. But I did not want to think about that. I was leaving, and there was no one on earth who could stop me from climbing on a bus and driving back across the border. No one on earth—not even Hank McKellar.

I went back to the cabin, packed my bags, then lugged them along the dock and into town. The mud of the streets came up to my ankles. I stopped in doorways, rested, then moved along again, scanning the street, watching for a tall body striding with a slight hunch to its strong shoulders. I was struggling toward freedom, and it seemed hours before I reached the two-story hotel.

The lobby was barren except for a few straight-back chairs. A wide door opened onto a combination bar, restaurant, and grocery store to one side of the tiny desk. A flight of wooden stairs climbed into darkness in a far corner. I put down the bag and approached the mustached clerk who dozed behind the desk.

"*Buenos dias.*" I groped for my college Spanish. "*Buenos dias, senor.*"

He coughed, raised his black head, and grinned at me with yellow teeth. "*Senorita?*"

"Bus?" I said. "*Collectivo?* Train? *Fer de Corille?* United States? California? You understand? *Compreno? Comprendez?*" I was rattled, mixing bad French with accurate Spanish, leaning over the desk with my knotted fist emphasizing each word by pounding down on the plywood counter. But the clerk only grinned. Freedom was slipping away, and gradually the hysteria rose inside me. I pounded my fist up and down, up and down. My voice rattled meaningless words, and helpless tears choked into my throat. "Please! *Por favor!* Please!" until I became terrified with the urgency of my own voice, and I leaned on the desk and merely stared foolishly into the grinning brown face. "Well," I said finally. "*Gracias, senor.*" And I turned helplessly back into the room—turned face to face with round little Mr. Petey in his rumpled Palm Beach suit.

"Good morning." Mr. Petey was smiling. "There are no buses, Mrs. Gwynn. I have a car, of course, but—" He shrugged, picked up my bags and waddled off toward the bar. "Come along. You could use some breakfast." I followed stupidly. I watched him set my bags by a marble-topped table, lay his hat on one wire chair, and wave a pudgy hand toward another. "You're hungry?"

"Yes, I—" I nodded my head violently. I laughed and sat down. The fear had gone out of me. I was bewildered, relaxed, tired. In my entire life I had never been so relieved at meeting anyone.

Mr. Petey was in no hurry about anything. He ordered onion rolls and coffee. He spoke beautiful Spanish, smiling as he waved his short arms. He talked about the weather. He said a storm was coming up. First the rain, now the wind, and by this afternoon a real gale. "So you see," he said, smiling, "you will not be sailing today at all."

I nodded, wondering how he knew so much, why he was not more concerned. The coffee and rolls came, and we ate for a moment without speaking. Mr. Petey nibbled on the roll like a fat rabbit. It took him a long time to finish. Then he wiped the crumbs from his fingers, lit a Mexican cigar, took a huge puff, looked at me, and said, "Now, Mrs. Gwynn—now we are at the end of a very long road. Things happen, Mrs. Gwynn. Many things happen. And now that I see you're about to leave Mr. McKellar, now maybe I can tell you about him." He paused and I waited. Then he spoke again, softly now, saying everything from the very beginning, some ten years before.

"Mr. Hank McKellar is quite a fellow, Mrs. Gwynn—and from a long way back. 1942, in fact. You were a child then, but McKellar—he was a very young officer in the Canadian navy."

"He told me—"

"The Canadian navy. On a destroyer. That was during the rough days of submarine warfare, and McKellar's ship was torpedoed in the North Atlantic. The captain and executive officer were killed. McKellar was first lieutenant, which put him in command. Well, he put out what rafts were left, and climbed into the only boat just as the destroyer was going down. Last to leave the ship and all that sort of thing. But the boat was way overcrowded, not enough food or water, and a heavy sea. No question that McKellar knew what was going on. Boat was going down. Overcrowded, you understand. Shipping water every second. Well, what does a man do? Depends on the man, you see. And McKeller—he threw everything he could over the side, and when that didn't help, he ordered certain men over the side to lighten the boat. When a man refused he threw him in personally. Quite a rough fellow, you know, even then, and—well, the point is, a rescue ship arrived almost immediately. See what that means? Understand the situation?"

"Yes." I shuddered and sipped at the strong coffee. "Yes...."

"Men deliberately murdered. One way to look at it. Lots of ways to look at it. Anyway, McKellar was court-martialed. Lots of trouble and all, though with a war on and with all those ways of looking at it, they tried to keep it out of the papers. But still—the families of those drowned men, you see—five in all—well, they did a little probing of their own, and McKellar was discharged. Maybe right, maybe wrong. I'm no moralist, Mrs. Gwynn. He did fine at the trial. A question of five men or forty. How did he know the rescue ship was so close? What would another man do? Very hardminded fellow, he is. Explained how he chose the men. All unmarried. None with fiancées. Not chosen by rank or position—just who loved and was loved, you see. McKellar was God. He decided who mattered and who didn't matter, to somebody else in this world."

Mr. Petey's cigar had gone out. He dropped the huge ash in his saucer and lit the cigar again. "Of course you see the point. McKellar wasn't married—not engaged either. So why not go overboard himself? Well, there you are. He's in command, isn't he? Last to leave the destroyer. Didn't get off till it sank right under his feet. So what's the difference in a life boat? He'd be the last to leave that too. Always the last to leave a ship, you see. Keep her afloat at any cost. Save all the men you can. But when your own son is deliberately drowned—then maybe you don't understand all that tradition business. Looks like McKellar's saving his own neck and all that sort of thing."

"Do you—" I swallowed and lit a cigarette. My brain was numb. I tried to understand, but it was too big and impossible to grasp. "Do you think he was saving himself?"

Mr. Petey shrugged. "Knowing McKellar's record, I'd say no. He's a tough man, but no coward. He figures what's right and does things that way and—there isn't anyone going to change him."

"I know," thinking that Hank felt we were right—he and I were right—and nothing could make him think different.

"Point is, of course," Mr. Petey went on, "he falsified the records when he joined our navy. Didn't change his name because of pride, you see. Insists on his own identity. But made false statements to get in the navy at all. Good reason, I suppose. Navy wouldn't have taken a man discharged from the Canadian navy, and McKellar—well, he insists on justifying himself. Only one way to do that. In war, Mrs. Gwynn. I understand McKellar's been a terror during this Korean thing. Plenty of nerve. Always wanting close quarters with the enemy. Trying to get into landing parties and force a situation, you see. Prove himself. Not just to other people, mostly to himself. Wants to wash away any creeping doubts from that tough, but not-quite-tough-enough mind of Lieutenant Hank McKellar."

"I see." I finished the coffee. It was bitter. I grimaced and laughed nervously. "So it's not serious, the reason you want him."

"Technical. We'll discharge him. Publicity. Disgrace. You know."

"Yes."

"He's not made for it."

"No."

"Couldn't take it."

"No, he couldn't."

"So he's running. Looking for a new opening and—" Mr. Petey paused, ran a hand over his chubby face. "And—he doesn't want to run alone."

I drew in my breath, then let it out slowly, avoiding Mr. Petey's eyes.

He was watching me. "None of my business, but—you're getting smart, Mrs. Gwynn. If you loved him—"

"I don't—not any more. I—I guess I never did."

His eyes flickered. "I knew that when I saw your bags. Situation like this, with a husband and all—it takes a lot of loving. Good you found it out."

"Yes." I wet my lips. Mr. Petey was making everything good for me, yet not loving Hank enough was a crime really. I should have known this end at the very beginning. I thought about it. I said, "But if I did love him—"

"None of this would make any difference."

"No, it wouldn't." I paused and raised my eyes to his. They were pale blue and watery behind his glasses. "I've made my own mistakes, Mr. Petey. What you told me doesn't change how I feel now or did feel then. It just puts some weight on what I suspected—a girl needs tenderness, and there's no *real* tenderness in Hank McKellar. He wants me and—"

"And as long as he thinks you belong together, he'll go to any lengths to keep it that way."

"I'm frightened. For the first time I'm really scared."

"Well—" Mr. Petey stood. He dropped a coin on the table and lifted my bags. "Let me keep the bags for you. Go back to the boat. Just go back, and I think you'll be surprised."

"I can't. I—"

"Tell McKellar it's no good. I promise you—swear to you—you'll always feel better for it."

"What—what he'll do, I—"

"I promise you'll be surprised."

I didn't understand. I looked at Mr. Petey's beaming face, and knew I trusted him. Yet I did not understand.

"Go on," he said. And he touched my arm. "Go on."

I found no words to say. I merely nodded and walked across the bar, moving dumbly, trying to pull everything together in my mind—exactly what I felt toward Hank, toward myself, toward Mr. Petey, toward the future, whatever that might be. I walked out of the hotel and through the mud, and did not notice the muck that seeped into my shoes. I felt the rising wind against my face and leaned into it with my mind on other things. The fishermen were still there on the dock. They watched me and laughed, but I paid no attention. I walked on to the boat that swung erratically in the wind.

The deck was clear, except for the neatly coiled ropes and the two white life preservers secured on either side of the cabin. Hank was below, or he had not returned from buying provisions. I stepped softly to the deck and listened with my ear against the hatch. But I heard nothing. Finally I pushed the hatch open carefully, and with my heart in my throat and a fierce terror eating away inside me, I descended the ladder to the cabin. My eyes found the figure sitting in Hank's bunk. I tried to cry out, but the words were stifled in my throat. I grasped the ladder for support and waited and waited. But the man only watched me with no expression whatsoever. He held Hank's revolver in one hand. It was pointed at my stomach. But the hand shook as I faced him, and he lowered the gun slowly to his lap.

There was terrible silence. The man wet his lips. My own mouth was dry and it was all I could do to say his name. "Phil." That one word. "Phil...."

CHAPTER TWENTY-ONE

T HERE WAS A VOICE and there was darkness. Then, after a
long time, reality swam back into focus. I was sitting on
the bottom rung of the ladder. A rough hand was on my arm.
But it pulled away sharply when my eyes opened, and I said the
word again, "Phil...." and pulled unsteadily to my feet. Phil had
jerked away. He stared at me. His eyes were still brown, his face
still square, his hair still black with the tight waves that curled
when they got wet. But he was thinner than I remembered. And I
watched his strong, square body as he braced himself against the
bunk. He looked out the porthole and said, "Are you all right?"
in a fiat, painful voice.

"Yes, I'm—all right," staring at him, trying to *know* that this
was Phil.

He pressed his nose against the glass. "That's good." His
breath made patterns on the closed porthole.

"Phil...."

"I suppose you're wondering how I got here."

"Yes, I—"

"A Mr. Petey. Contacted me the minute I got off the plane in
Frisco. He seemed to know a lot about you."

"Yes—he does."

"Didn't ask any questions. But I've done a lot of figuring for
myself. At the Top-of-the-Mark. Went up there the first night and
did some figuring. Looked out at the city and remembered—" He
straightened and his hand found the tin cup lying empty on the

bunk. He picked it up, flung it to the deck, and stamped on it with his heel. He swore and looked at me. There was no anger in his eyes. Just bewildered pain. "Oh God!" he said. "Oh, my God!"

"Listen, Phil—"

"I don't get it. I don't get it, I just don't get it!"

"Neither do I." I stood. I wanted to touch him. I wanted to cry with his arms around me. But I could not reach him.

He must have known, but still he remained hard and horribly detached. "Well—I just wanted to make sure. See for myself."

"I'm not staying here, Phil. I was going to find you—try to explain—"

He laughed.

"My bags are already at the hotel."

"Nothing to explain. So where you going now? Reno?"

"No. I don't know."

"Sadler Falls?"

"I don't know."

"I suppose Reno's the best. No sense dragging this thing around the courts."

"Look, Phil—"

"I've looked. What am I supposed to do now? What the hell am I supposed to say?"

"I don't know." I sat slowly on the bunk. "It would take forever to say it all. I don't think you could ever understand—not what I feel, but why I did it. But now you're back, it's like—well, like nothing's happened at all."

"Just a gay little excursion." He was sarcastic, and laughed bitterly.

"Not so gay, Phil. Really not so ..." I paused and remembered Hank was probably on his way here now. The fear returned, and I said, "We'd better get out of here, Phil. Both of us. Never mind about what's between us. We'd better get out of here. Hank will be coming back and—"

"And I'll kill the bastard!" He picked up the revolver from the bunk. He cocked it, and the click was loud in the cabin.

A cold chill ran down my spine. I stumbled toward him, saying, "Look, Phil, you don't know him—listen to what I ..." Then I paused again and stood uncertainly in the center of the cabin. Something was wrong, but I did not know exactly what. I listened, but heard nothing. The boat still swung gently beneath us. The wind still howled above. But something flopped and something creaked, and then the boat no longer rolled, but seemed to list gently to one side. I turned and knelt on the bunk. I peered through the porthole and saw the dock some hundred yards behind us and Mr. Petey standing there in the wind with his pants whipping against his chubby legs. He was shouting. He flapped his arms as though trying to fly. Then his fat body turned and he puffed back down the dock, shouting to someone I could not see.

Phil turned from the other porthole. "We're moving," he said.

"Hank!"

"The son-of-a-bitch!" He gripped the gun in his fist, slipped off the safety, and started for the ladder. I caught his arm as he reached the first rung. I held on and talked frantically, trying to stop him. He tried to shake me loose, but I grabbed his shirt then, still talking, saying, "He doesn't know you're here, and you don't know him, you don't *know* him, and he doesn't know you're here!"

"He'll find out."

"Listen, Phil, I'll go up. See what's going on." I held tight to his sleeve and kept talking crazily. He looked at me, his eyes full of hate, then sat in the bunk once more. He was trembling with rage. His hands kept playing with the gun, flipping the safety on and off. He laughed and swore, and watched me as I climbed the ladder and pushed open the hatch. As I closed it behind me, I looked back at Phil's face. It was no longer angry. It was dead now. He tried to laugh, and his mouth tried to speak. Something about my going to Hank. Something about to hell with both of us.

Hank was at the wheel. He was hunched forward with the spokes braced under his arm. His face was covered with water. His hair was plastered down against his head. He looked at me calmly and grinned and said, "Sorry, baby, but I had to pull out in a hurry. Not even time to store the provisions." He nodded to a large box of groceries in the cockpit. "Our Mr. Petey is a persistent kind of guy."

"I know...."

"I saw you leave him in the hotel." He was shouting over the wind.

"Yes, he told me about you. Everything."

"And you came back anyway." He stared directly at me. The look in his eyes meant one thing—finally we were together; nothing could ever separate us.

The wind had risen since we'd left the tiny bay. It howled through the rigging, pitched us from side to side so it took all Hank's strength to keep the boat on course.

"Hank!" I shouted above the wind.

"Don't worry, baby! We'll make it! I'm telling you—"

"Turn back, Hank !"

"You're kidding."

"Turn back!" I stumbled toward him, fell to my knees, and clutched at his arm. He must have thought I was frightened by the high waves, for he pushed me away gently, saying something about the raging sea, and how much he loved it. But I crawled back again through the water that slopped into the cockpit. He held me off with one arm, steered with the other. All the time he kept shouting, "We'll make it, we'll make it!" laughing sometimes, thrilled by the wind and the storm around us. I let go his arm and clung to the gunwale, half-lying now, my own hair in wet strings about my face. I heard his laughter and saw his face and knew that Hank McKellar was finally at home. A boat and a gale, me at his feet and himself at the helm. He'd been born for this. He was finally at home.

Minutes passed. Hank concentrated on sailing the boat. I lay propped against the stern, gasping into the howling wind. Neither of us spoke. I saw the mainland in the distance now, and almost straight ahead a small sandy island. We were running toward it, heading through the waves, then veering sharply, gliding along the trough now, so the boat rocked with sickening lurches. The sails came about, then the boom swung hard and the canvas snapped open again with a terrifying crack. But Hank was still laughing. Laughing and shouting, "Just coming around, baby, and we're on our way, baby, on our way!"

Finally I heard the laughter fade. I saw his eyes widen, and the muscles tighten along his jaw. His mouth dropped open, then snapped shut again viciously. He swore violently, and I swung around to the hatchway behind me.

Phil had appeared at the top of the ladder. He stepped down to the cockpit, slid the hatch shut behind him, braced himself against it, and stared at Hank with hate in his eyes and his body taut, tensed as though ready to spring. The gun was in his hand. It was pointed straight at Hank's face.

For a moment Hank was thrown off balance. But confidence returned immediately. "What the hell!" he shouted. "What the hell!" His eyes swung to me, to Phil, back to me again. I said nothing, but my lips moved dumbly, forming the words, *Phil* and *husband*. Hank stared at me, then started laugh-ing. It was hysterical laughter, interspersed with words screamed at Phil. "You're too late, soldier! You're too late! Get it? Get it?" On and on. This was *his* boat and *his* storm. He was king. I was *his* woman, and Phil was a ridiculous outsider, blundering into a situation over which he had no control.

"What you going to do?" Hank screamed. "Got any ideas? Any ideas? Think you can pull that trigger and handle this boat yourself? Think you can handle this girl yourself?" And he laughed again and looked at me, still laughing, still laughing. But this time his eyes clung, and this time the laughter was raised on the wind and carried out across the sea. My eyes stung with salt, so I could scarcely see his face. But I kept staring at him through the wet gray haze as I crawled backward until I touched Phil's legs. Then I pulled myself upright beside him, so that we stood there together with our backs against the cabin—the two of us together, looking into Hank's crazy eyes. He scowled back at us. His mouth twitched. His eyes blazed. And then something went from his face, and I knew then that it had happened.

Something snapped inside Hank's brain. His hand slipped from the wheel. He rose to his full height. He snarled and sprang at Phil with his arms outstretched, a wild roar emerg-ing from his throat. Phil met him squarely in the center of the cockpit. They swung together, swearing, slipping on the wet boards. The wheel spun crazily and the boat swung around and wallowed in toward the tiny island some two hundred yards away. The boom hung motionless for one uncertain moment. Then the wind filled the sail and the boom came hard across the boat, straight into the struggling bodies, knocking them down. As they fell, a huge wave hurled the boat into the air. It came down with the crash of splintering wood. It shuddered and heaved to its side.

The jarring stop flung me back to the deck, into the two prostrate bodies. Phil lay motionless, knocked unconscious by the swinging boom. He lay beside me, face down, his arms spread wide. Hank lay struggling, half sprawled across my body. His face was inches from mine, his eyes looking into me and through me. He pulled himself to a sitting position and his hands reached toward me. Swearing, he clutched at my blouse and ripped it from my shoulders. His cold hands pressed frantically into my bare back and his face came even closer. He spoke between his teeth, digging his fingers into my flesh.

"You love me! God damn it, you love me, you love me, you love me!" He dug his fingers into my back each time he said it. I winced but did not answer. The boat was swinging crazily on the reef beneath us.

Hank's face dripped with water. Blood ran down from a cut on the side of his head. He jerked a hand from under me, ran it hard over my stomach and bare breasts, up along my chest and throat. The strong fingers closed on my throat, stiffened, then relaxed slowly, very slowly, while his eyes seemed to glaze over. "Don't love me, don't love me," he mumbled. He laughed jerkily. He stared down at my half-naked body, then put out a hand and pulled my blouse over me once more, saying, "Don't love me," and pulled himself upright.

Still I did not move. I looked up and saw him standing tall above me. His shirt was ripped. The blood ran down his face and neck. He was a giant against the gray sky. For a long moment he stood that way, towering over me, frowning, considering. Then suddenly he jerked away. He laughed and moved forward. I turned my head and saw him clamber onto the deck beside the mast, hang onto a wire stay with one hand while he unfastened a life preserver from the side of the cabin with the other. He tossed the round white preserver into the cockpit, then went for the second preserver on the port side. The boat had listed far over by now. The entire port rail was under water, and waves pounded in against me on the cockpit's deck.

I crawled to Phil and held his head above the water while Hank threw the second preserver at my feet, then leaped down beside me. His face was almost unrecognizable. He worked with the fury of a man gone completely mad. He yanked me to my feet. I struggled, hitting out at him, but he held me tight and laughed crazily while he jammed the life preserver around me. Phil was gaining consciousness then. He struggled to his feet, still weak from the blow on his head. But Hank pushed him down again.

"You bastard," he muttered. "All right, you bastard." He picked up the second preserver, pulled it over Phil's feet and up under his arms. Then he lifted him from the deck, swore again, and heaved him, weak and dazed, over the side and into the boiling sea. For a moment Phil disappeared from sight. Then he rose, a blob of white, his head above water as the monstrous waves rushed him in toward the sandy beach.

Hank turned to me. He was laughing again. "So you love him, don't you? So he loves you, doesn't he? Thrown people over the side before, you know. Heard about that, didn't you? Petey told you about that. Pick 'em up and heave 'em in, and McKellar's the last man to leave his ship." The wild laughter broke and trailed away. He yanked me to my feet, clutched my arms in the steel grip of his hands, and suddenly, for just one single moment, he was the Hank McKellar I had wanted—the Hank McKellar for whom I would have destroyed my very life. His voice was low—rough, but low—and I could have sworn that he was crying.

"Goodbye," he said. "So long, baby." Then he swore and lifted me clear and lowered me gently into the raging sea. I was swept away almost immediately. But the preserver kept my head above water, and I could see Hank's eyes-still watching me—gray eyes, with the tears or the salt water staining the blood on his cheek. For a moment I could see him—every inch of him—a man come full circle, who lives and dies by his own convictions.

Then the face was gone. I saw only his back as he turned and shouted across the water to a power boat that crawled toward us from a quarter mile away. "Come on, Petey!" he screamed. "Here I am, Petey! Last man to leave the ship, Petey! You can tell 'em about that! Tell 'em all about that—all about that!" And his figure seemed to loom bigger now than the boat itself, taller than the mast, larger than the sea and the gray sky above. Then suddenly the boat went down and the great figure went under with it, sliding, slipping, almost gracefully, into the churning sea.

CHAPTER TWENTY-TWO

M INUTES PASSED. Minutes or hours. And the sea rushed on, lifting me from trough to wave, from trough to wave. Before me the beach grew larger, whiter, until in a moment I was balanced high above it, high over Phil's prostrate figure, then the surf flung me down hard against the wet sand. I felt the backwash sucking at my legs, trying frantically to pull me back as I clutched at the sand and pulled myself painfully up the beach where I dropped again, exhausted, my arms wide, my blouse torn completely from me, my hair matted with sand and gravel, my hands and knees cut and bleeding. I lay there motionless for a long time. Then finally strength returned. I raised my head and saw Mr. Petey's power boat moving ever closer to the beach. I saw Phil's body only yards away. He was struggling to sit up. His clothes were torn, and he was bleeding from a cut on his forehead. His glazed eyes turned in my direction, but he still did not move.

I started toward him. The sand scraped my naked breasts. It dug into the open wounds so that I wanted to scream. I bit down on my lips until the taste of blood mixed with the salt. I prayed and struggled on, while Phil still watched me. Only a few yards now. Red fire burst inside my brain. "Phil...." I moaned. "Phil—I'm coming, Phil. I'm coming, Phil—"

And somehow in all that horror, as I crawled on across the beach, I knew that now and tomorrow and next month and next year Phil would still be waiting, watching me with his hurt brown eyes, yet waiting all the same. For it was up to me. The long crawl back was up to me.

THE END

www.ingramcontent.com/pod-product-compliance
Lightning Source LLC
Chambersburg PA
CBHW030256270626
47156CB00022B/2788

* 9 7 8 1 9 6 2 8 9 6 4 9 8 *